Mentoring Maye

A BOMBSHELLS OF BRENTWOOD NOVEL BY
VICTORIA BLUE

Mentoring Maye

A BOMBSHELLS OF BRENTWOOD NOVEL BY

VICTORIA BLUE

WATERHOUSE PRESS

For David,

the person who's taught me more about

love and life than anyone.

CHAPTER ONE

MAYE

"No, really, Joel. I promise it's nothing you're doing," I tried explaining again. Then quickly added, "Or not doing. There's nothing to work on or improve upon. Seriously, I know it sounds so cliché, but it's me."

Breaking up with a person who just wasn't ready to let go was never easy. But this sweet relationship had run its course, and I was ready to move on.

I needed to move on.

In a perfect world, this conversation would've ended ten minutes prior, but instead, here we were. My trying to convince the guy he didn't have a laundry list of shortcomings, and his making every promise to do better. Try harder. But wasn't that the underlying theme to this whole situation? You weren't supposed to have to try when it was meant to be.

And this whole relationship was taking way more effort than I had to give.

"But your dad and I were supposed to go fishing," he finally croaked as if it would change things. And if I wasn't mistaken, tears were being shed now too.

"You can still do that. Nothing says we can't still be friends," I said, trying to placate the man.

"Be serious," he scoffed. And yes, it was definitely through

1

tears.

"I'm going to let you go before one of us says something hurtful," I announced. I'd been on this end of these conversations enough times in my life to know we had just reached the tipping point. Next he'd lash out, say all the things he'd always wanted to say but was sparing my feelings by not. Or that would be his heroic reason for avoiding the venom up to that point.

"I wish you nothing but the best, Joel. Good night." After disconnecting the call, I turned the ringer off too in case he called back. One too many attempts, and my sister who shared the same bedroom would snatch the phone and give the guy a real tongue-lashing.

It was her superpower, after all.

But when I looked across the room to the now empty bed, I realized she'd dipped on me at some point. Couldn't exactly blame her. The conversation had made me sick too.

Well, now that that was out of the way, time to get down to homework. I was working on my final project for the last class before summer break and quickly running out of steam. This class hadn't been interesting or challenging, but most of them weren't. School felt like rowing a boat with one oar.

Circles.

There was potential excitement on the horizon, though. I had landed an internship for the summer months and started in less than a week. My dad was heartbroken that I hadn't accepted the opportunity with the firm he worked for, but honestly, I wanted to do something on my own for a change.

Being from a large family had its perks, but there were some drawbacks too. One of the major ones being I never felt like an individual. I was always just one of the Farsey girls.

To make matters worse, I was a twin. Don't get me wrong—I loved my sister with my entire being, but living life as half of a whole could really suck. There was a point in my early teens that I swore if one more person asked me, "Which one are you?" I would've become a felon.

Those years are hard for every girl. Learning about yourself and where you fit into the world complicates every situation and every decision. As a twin, it was automatically assumed you were interchangeable with your sibling, so the fight to be seen as an individual just made everything worse.

And again, I adored my sister and applauded all her life choices so far. But she and I were as different as oil and vinegar. And lately, her personality had been as acidic as that condiment, too. Something was definitely bothering her—and I was talking at a bone-deep level—but every time I asked her, she'd clam up. I figured she'd open up to me or one of our other sisters when she was ready.

Just as I was thinking those thoughts, Shepperd came back into our room with a huge sports jug filled with water. I honestly couldn't remember the last time I saw her eat.

"That was painful to listen to," she said with a magnificent eye roll.

I had to agree. "You should've been on the actual call." Plopping down on the edge of my bed, I cradled my face in my palms. Being mean to people had always been difficult for me. My twin, however, seemed to excel at it. The breakup was long overdue, but having to listen to a man grovel was on my top ten things to avoid at all costs.

"You're better off without him," she growled and burrowed into the nest of blankets on her bed. "He wasn't good enough for you. No one will ever be."

She mumbled that last part, and it made me smile. No matter what her mood toward everyone else, we always had our own special thing.

"Shep?" I called so she wouldn't doze off. The girl could fall asleep faster than anyone I knew.

She made some sort of noise, so I tiptoed into a minefield of topics I knew she hated. "Have you eaten today? Actual food, I mean?"

"Maye, don't."

"I'm worried about you. You can't make me stop, either." I stuck my tongue out when she peeked a single eye from below the covers.

"I had a protein shake when I got home from the gym," she muttered.

"That's it? All day? How about if I go make some popcorn? Will you share it with me? You can tell me about your finals today," I offered hopefully.

She whipped the covers down so I could see her entire face and admitted, "I didn't go."

"Didn't you have chem today?" I asked, knowing damn well she did. Like always, I memorized her schedule and mine the moment we got them. These twin habits were hard to break, no matter how much I complained about them.

"Yeah, I'll talk to the professor and see if I can do a makeup. The guy hates me and gives me shitty grades no matter how hard I try. It's a waste of time. All of it is."

I went over to her side of the room and lifted her blankets. "Move over," I announced while lifting a leg to the mattress to climb in beside her. She would bitch at first, but we always snuggled together when something was wrong, and I never wanted that to stop.

"No. Get in your own bed. I'm sleeping."

So I switched on the whiny voice she hated. "Let me in. I want to snuggle."

"No, Maye," she huffed and pushed my hip. "Get." But then, just like the last time, and the time before that, she moved to the center of her mattress and made room for me beside her. "You're such a pain in the ass," she griped.

I smiled into the pillow. "Am not."

"Are too. And I thought you were making popcorn?" she asked.

That made me sit up. "Do you want some?" I asked hopefully.

She shrugged like she wasn't truly starving. "I'd eat a few pieces."

I was on my feet in a second and grabbing my robe off the hook on the back of our door. "I'll be right back. Don't fall asleep, or I'll just wake you," I warned before I turned and hustled out to the kitchen.

It was just us and our youngest sister, Clemson, at home with our parents now. Our oldest sister, Hannah, married and was expecting her first baby. Any day now, actually. I missed having her around the house but was so happy she found true love and was starting a family. That little girl was going to be the most spoiled baby ever born!

Our second-oldest sister, Agatha, was also newly married and living with her husband. What a story that relationship was! But that man was so good for her, and they were adorable together. She had been on a self-destructive path when they'd met, so I was silently thankful he came into her life when he did.

And not that she needed a man to save her, but she did

need someone to get through her stubborn, beautiful, blond head that she was worthy of all the good things in life. We all were.

If I could somehow get that same message through to my twin, I'd be the family hero. That wasn't a role I actively sought out, but everyone was concerned about Shepperd for one reason or another. I knew the truth, though. Most of her bitterness was an act to keep people at arm's length. But this starving bullshit had to stop.

Back in our room with a delightfully buttery, salty bowl of goodness, I proclaimed, "I'm back! Sit up, and I'll brush your hair."

"I don't want my hair brushed," she grumbled from her nest.

"Too bad. Up." I pulled on the blankets, and she gripped the edge tighter.

"I'm freezing. It's always so damn cold in this house. Between Mother's hot flashes and Dad's general insanity, they keep it way too cold. I swear I can see my breath in the morning."

Shep sat up, and I placed the bowl in her lap before crawling onto her bed and settling in behind her. Her hair was as long as mine but even thicker. Lately, though, it always looked lifeless and stringy, and I knew it was because of her bad nutrition habits.

I found her brush on her nightstand and started working through the mass one section at a time. "You shouldn't go to bed with it wet. Look at all these knots," I advised as I worked.

"Maye. I'm serious. Stop nagging me about, well, shit, about everything. I was exhausted from my workout and just wanted to lie down."

"Toss me a piece. Let's see if I can catch it," I told her instead of agreeing to stop mothering her. She threw a piece in my direction before I could prepare, and the kernel bounced off my cheek and landed on the blanket.

I giggled. "Wait till I'm ready, at least."

"So how was class for you? Glad to be out for the summer?" she asked, and I smiled behind her. I knew she'd start chatting eventually. I just didn't understand why she always made me fight through her defenses first.

"Definitely glad I didn't enroll in anything for the summer session. I'm anxious to find out more about the internship, though. I have a one-on-one with Professor Chaplin tomorrow morning. Now that I got rid of Joel too, I feel so light. So free."

"I can't imagine what that would feel like," she muttered under her breath, but I caught every word. I'd play dumb for a little and see if she'd open up more.

"I thought you and that dude weren't exclusive. Is he getting clingy?" I asked, even though I knew the answer.

"What dude? Marcus? Shit, sister. Keep up. I got rid of him like a month ago. And yes, he got way too clingy, way too fast." She was quiet for a minute while I tugged at a stubborn tangle.

"There's this guy at the gym, though," she started, but left me hanging there.

"Go on," I encouraged. "Don't just leave me with no other details."

"Don't have much to tell. We've just been giving each other the eye every time we see each other. Lately he's there almost every time I am. I think he changed his schedule to match mine. It seems too coincidental."

This was the most animated I'd seen her in a long time.

This would be a good topic to go back to when she got angry about other things she didn't want to discuss. And these days, there were so many that it was hard to keep track of them all.

"Tell me all about him," I insisted.

"I just told you. We haven't even spoken. We just eye-fuck across the gym," she said in a frustrated tone. But then added, "Definitely makes the workout time go quicker."

"Well, describe him to me. What does he look like? How old would you guess?" I peppered her with questions.

"I'm sure he's older than us. Probably upwards of ten years. He has that man look about him, you know what I mean? No trace of boy left. Anywhere."

"Mmm, okay. I'm liking the sound of this so far. I've always thought you'd do better with an older guy. Older than us, I mean. I'm not talking in his fifties or anything like that, but maybe like twenty-eight to thirty-two."

She turned to eye me skeptically over her shoulder. "Did you really just pull that out of your ass, or do you give my love life that much consideration?"

I answered honestly, "No, I've really thought about this before. I think you are way more mature than people our age. You need someone who will stimulate you."

"Hell yes, I do!" she said with a dark laugh.

We all had throaty laughs, genetically gifted to us from our mother. But Shepperd's always had this sinister edge to it that made it deeper and darker.

Playfully, I smacked her shoulder. "That's not what I meant. Though there is merit to the thought," I said while pressing the end of the brush to my chin, pretending to give it deep consideration.

"He has really dark hair. It's definitely black, but it's so dark and shiny, it looks wet half the time. And it's super thick and wavy. Kind of longer, like it could be messy in an instant."

"And you've not even said hello?"

"Nope. Now and then we give each other a little nod. He smiled at me today, which made me instantly run and hide in the locker room," she admitted. "Such an idiot," my twin mumbled into the cradle of her palms.

"This is so exciting. We have to find out who he is!" I said, getting into the mystery of it all.

Instantly she became defensive. "What do you mean *we*? Just don't worry about it."

"Aww, come on. Let me live vicariously through you. Now that I'm single, I need an outlet for my romantic notions."

"Well, matchmake for Clemmie. I'm not looking for a guy right now, and I think I heard her and that dipshit she's been dragging around arguing tonight. Who needs the drama and complications, you know?" she said, chewing thoughtfully on the few pieces of popcorn she finally put in her mouth.

"What time are you going next? I want to go along," I persisted. It would never happen, though. I hated going to the gym.

"I'm not telling you. God, I'd be so embarrassed. Don't make me regret telling you," she warned. "Then the whole twin thing would start," she said, and I felt her whole body stiffen.

"I'm only teasing. Calm down." I brushed her hair back and worked it into a single braid down the center of her back. "There. Now it won't be crazy in the morning," I announced while surveying my handiwork.

My sister fingered the thick braid and said, "Thanks, Maye. Now get out of my bed." She held out the bowl as I stood. "Take this with you. The smell is starting to nauseate me."

"I'll go put the rest away. Or maybe Dad will want it. I'm ready for bed. You?"

She sank deeper into her stack of pillows and bitched, "I was ready an hour ago."

"Night, sister. I love you," I said and kissed the top of her head—the only part still exposed to the room air.

"Night, Mayday."

It didn't escape my attention that at some point about a year ago, my twin stopped telling all of us she loved us. And it was a sentiment we had all exchanged freely our whole lives. Eventually she'd open up to me and tell me what was going on, but I knew with Shepperd it had to be on her time.

I just wished that time would come so she'd be the happy, vibrant, creative, and fun young woman she used to be.

CHAPTER TWO

MAYE

Bright and early the next morning, I scrambled down the hall to claim the shower before anyone else set up base camp in there. Imagine sharing one bathroom between five girls. Luckily, we were typically in different stages of school while growing up, so we had different start times. It had to have been incredibly difficult on our mom, who shuttled us all to and from school every day, but she never complained. When she said we were her whole life, she meant it to her core.

I reminded myself to be grateful for the things I had instead of focusing on the negative. It was the way I started every morning, and it generally set the tone for a positive, feel-good kind of day.

My nerves were pretty jangled because I was about to find out how I'd be spending my summer. Professor Chaplin wasn't a nice man in class, so I had no idea what to expect in our private conference. He hand-selected internships for his students based on a lengthy questionnaire he had us fill out at the beginning of the semester and then again about halfway through.

While rinsing my hair, I tried to remember what was asked on that questionnaire. I could only come up with a few basic things about our demographics, though, so instead of the shower relaxing me, I felt worse than when I got in.

I decided to go with a casual look for our meeting. Originally I planned on a smart business suit and pumps, but my sister said it looked like I was playing dress-up in my mom's clothes. Not the impression I was going for, so I changed my whole approach and picked a long, flowing skirt with a large blue-and-white floral print. A plain white T-shirt that I pulled tight around my small waist and tied into a knot at my lower back topped the outfit. I slid my feet into one of my favorite pairs of sandals on the way out the door and hopped in the car my twin and I shared, giving myself plenty of time to get to campus.

When Shepperd came skulking out to the car, I was confused. She tried the passenger side door, but it was locked. After I opened it, she slid into the front seat beside me and tossed her gym bag through the space between us and into the back seat. Luckily I was watching her, or I would've been smacked in the side of the face and head with the colossal thing.

"Shep? What are you doing? I need to be on campus in thirty minutes. We talked about this last night."

"I have to work later. If I don't go to the gym now, I'll have to skip it altogether."

Trying to understand the logistics of both of us needing the car, I said, "But I don't know how long this is going to take. Can't you just borrow Mom's car for the day? Or God forbid, skip the gym?"

"Why should I give up my plans?" she asked stubbornly. "Just drop me off on your way. You can pick me up when you're done."

"That could be hours from now. And your gym is in the opposite direction of school. You know this," I replied, trying to keep the agitation I was feeling out of my tone and failing miserably.

She buckled her seat belt and instructed, "Just drive, Maye. Or switch with me and I'll drive. The sooner we get moving, the more time you'll have, regardless of who's behind the wheel," she said while staring straight ahead. Apparently she wasn't giving up on this plan.

So I coasted down our long driveway and headed toward my school. I wouldn't dare be late for this meeting. Professor Chaplin was an unfriendly guy. I didn't get the impression he'd sit around waiting for a late student or take too kindly to a student wasting his time with tardiness.

Shepperd finally looked up from her phone after about two miles into our drive.

"Maye? What the hell? You went the wrong way," she criticized.

"I'm not going to be late for this, Shep. You know Chaplin. He's likely to cancel the whole internship if I'm late." I shot a quick glance her way to see if she was listening. After she nodded, I proceeded to share my plan with her. "You can have the car when we get to school. I'll find something to do on campus until you're done working out. Just text me when you're heading back my way."

"Done," she replied while texting feverishly.

"Who are you talking to?" I asked, fully intruding into her business. "Is it the guy from the gym?"

"No one," she said and quickly closed the screen as if I could simultaneously read her messages and drive.

"I can't see your screen from here. Plus, I'm driving," I reassured her. "I was just curious."

"Or nosy," she mumbled.

"Well, that too." I laughed in agreement. After a few quiet minutes, I asked again. "So who were you texting?"

But she ignored me until her phone vibrated again. Then she went back to tapping away. I wouldn't ask again and risk having my head bitten off. Not before going into this meeting with my professor. I needed to be calm, cool, and collected. Fighting with my sister always left me wrung out.

We pulled up to the building where the teaching staff held office hours, and I put the car into park.

"Okay, so text me when you're on your way back, and I'll meet you here. Cool?" I knew I sounded like a neurotic parent, but she was notorious for blowing people off or simply forgetting what she'd agreed to.

"Yes. I'll meet you here. Good luck." She offered a fist for me to bump, but I was so floored by her kind words, I just stared at her in disbelief.

"Or not..." she said bitterly and dropped her hand.

"No, no. Seriously, sorry. That just took me by surprise. C'mon. I'll bump your fist, Shep." Now I was begging, and I scoffed at how ridiculous I sounded. I hated that her mood swings always had the rest of us on eggshells.

My sister got in the driver's seat and slammed the door. Without another word, she sped off before I hit the first step that led up to the majestic front doors. I loved this campus and all its history. Some of the classes were absolute shit, but the grounds and buildings always made me feel at home.

The man I was about to meet with did not, however. Dr. Andrew Chaplin was a mysterious professor. He never went out of his way to be likeable or even approachable. He certainly wasn't one of those instructors who hung around after class to offer extra help or information.

He was a by-the-rules kind of guy from day one. If you needed further instruction in his class, you could request a tutor or meet with him during his scheduled office hours. I was shocked when I got his email regarding this meeting because I thought his teacher's aide typically handled the summer internship assignments.

This was my first time in this particular building, so I was unfamiliar with the location of his office. Fortunately, there was a marquee in the lobby that listed who occupied each office. I found his name and office number and headed upstairs to the second floor. Of course, his office was the last one at the end of a very long hallway, and the heels on my sandals click-clacked the entire way.

Just as I was about to open his door, someone called my name from the other end of the corridor. When I swung around to see who was shouting in the otherwise silent building, I completely deflated.

"Joel." I paused, not wanting to deal with him right now. While he hustled the length of the hallway toward me, I muttered an unenthused, "Hey."

"I thought I saw you driving near the quad," he said excitedly and thumbed over his shoulder toward that area of campus. "But I realized it was Shepperd and flagged her down. She said she dropped you off, and I remembered you mentioned a meeting with Chaplin. Have you been in to see him yet?" He punctuated his rapid-fire question spree with a boyish grin.

Christ, what did I ever see in this guy?

That whole data dump pulled me up short because I had an excellent memory and nowhere in a quick scan of the last few days could I recall telling Joel about this meeting. I smelled a rat, and if I found out my twin sent this dipshit up here just to mess with me, I'd be giving her the silent treatment for a week.

Modulating my voice to blend a bit more with the vibe of the setting, I quietly began to whisper my reply. "Listen, I don't want to be late."

With an outstretched hand on the knob, I was about to tell him we could catch up later, but the door was pulled open from the inside, and Professor Chaplin loomed in the doorway with a disapproving scowl.

"If you don't mind, this isn't the social quad. Some of us are trying to work," he hissed bitterly.

"Oh, sorry. You're right. I— I— Uhh..." I stammered like a fool while Joel began backing away. Freaking coward was going to hightail it out of there and not even own up to the fact he was the one making all the noise.

"Ms. Farsey, I believe we have a meeting scheduled?" Dr. Chaplin asked. He gave Joel a once-over and said, "Run along, son. You can talk to your girlfriend when she's done here."

I stepped across the threshold while explaining, "He's not my boyfriend. Honestly, I don't know what he wanted. I was just about—"

He stopped me with a raised hand. "None of that concerns me," he said dryly and took the seat behind his desk in the cramped space. There was a plain folder and two pencils in the center of the desk and nothing else. Not even a laptop. Bookshelves lined the wall behind him, and my eyes darted from title to title on the perfectly aligned spines.

The dude had an eclectic selection for sure, but I was tongue-tied after the whole Joel scene to comment about any of them. Since I was an avid reader, it could've been a way to break the ice with the man, but the opportunity was gone before I could gather my wits.

"Sit down," he instructed, and I dropped gracelessly into the uncomfortable wooden chair. The back was mounted on a semicircle of spindles, which dug into my spine when I leaned back.

"You applied for an internship with the grant-writing program. Is that correct?" he asked while boring a hole in the center of my forehead with his dark, intense stare.

"Yes, that's correct. I'm excited to find—" I began to answer, but the man cut me off again.

"You've been chosen to work directly with me for the next ten weeks. I'm applying for three separate grants on behalf of the psychology department and require assistance. Your performance, attendance, and tested knowledge will compose your final grade in my class and can secure a scholarship within our graduate program here at the university. Do you have any questions?"

"Umm, noooo, I don't think so." This was the last thing I expected to hear today and wasn't sure I could handle an entire summer with this jerk. "Not at this time, at least," was my initial response, but I quickly started formulating a host of them, though. "Okay, actually, how many other interns will be working on these grants besides me?"

"It's a one-on-one learning opportunity, Ms. Farsey. You were selected by the professors of the department for the position, so I suggest you seriously consider the offer as the privilege it is."

Thankfully, my brain came back online, and I asked an important question rather than blurt out any one of the *What the fuck?* types that were clogging up the works in there.

"Thank you." I forced a smile through clenched teeth. "When do you need my decision?"

"Friday, five o'clock. We have a lot of work to accomplish, so if you aren't going to take the spot, I'll still have to interview other candidates."

"Not that this was an interview," I muttered and immediately regretted letting that slip out. When I met his icy glare, I knew he had heard me.

A quick grin sneaked out from his guarded features, but he reined it back in so fast I questioned if it had happened. "No, I suppose it wasn't." He didn't offer anything after that, so silence ballooned between us.

He stood from his much more comfortable chair, and I automatically rose as well. Apparently, our noninterview was over, and I was being dismissed.

"A word of advice, Ms. Farsey," Dr. Chaplin began, and I raised a brow with curiosity about what he had to offer. "If you do accept the position"—he paused until I nodded—"leave the boyfriend at home."

"He's not my boyfriend," I said for the second time, knowing full well the man didn't care what my response was. But my upbringing automatically kicked in, and I offered him my hand to shake. "Thank you for the opportunity. I'll be in touch."

There was no way I would walk out of that office like a scolded puppy. I felt triumphant to have had the last word. But my bravado crumbled when the door clapped shut right behind me as I left.

My whole body trembled, and I was furious with myself for letting that guy get under my skin. I was even more frustrated with the man himself for acting like such a dick. If he didn't like me, why personally choose me for the spot? Did I really want to spend the next ten weeks in an uncomfortable environment?

CHAPTER THREE

ANDREW

I held my breath until the infuriating clacking from her sandals was no longer perceivable from the empty hallway. But her alluring scent was still there when I finally inhaled again. That perfume she wore—day in and day out. It would drive any man insane. It was mystifying how the woman didn't have a trail of desperate suitors following her everywhere she went instead of just one loser who accompanied her to my door.

Similarly mystifying was how I willed my cock to stay flaccid while she sat directly across from me in my cramped office. I had to be the world's biggest glutton for punishment offering her the internship. If there were any sort of divine power in the universe, it would have intervened and swayed her to decline the opportunity. At the same time, we would have both been protected from the raw lust that ignited in my body in her presence.

I'd been teaching for eight years. It was never my intention to land here in my career path, but, well, here I was. Never, and I truly meant ever, had I been attracted to a student. Faculty knew what a tangled web it was to engage with students outside the classroom. In fact, when I was hired at this university years ago, there was an entire day of orientation devoted to not fucking around with your students.

Maybe a refresher course was in order.

★ ★ ★

Two days went by with no word from Ms. Farsey. Twice I had composed email messages reminding her I was awaiting her response, and twice I regained my sanity before sending the messages. But now I was getting pissed because the woman had me tied up in knots and didn't even know it. She would never know it. But if she refused the position, I was in for the longest summer of my life. If she accepted, it might actually be worse.

She'd be a complete fool to turn me down. There was so much I could teach her that would secure her place in the graduate program. I thought surely it would sway her decision when I added the scholarship icing to the cake. Yet here I still sat. Waiting. Waiting to get a message from a woman who was at least fifteen years my junior, likely more.

I'd been fighting the urge to snoop in her personal files in the school's system, but if she made me wait much longer, I could find out where she lived and go pay her a visit.

"Get a fucking grip, man," I mumbled beneath my breath. I was thinking like a horny boy, and enough was enough. If Maye Farsey was too much of a snob to realize the gift I was offering her, I'd move on to the next candidate.

The problem was, she was truly the best qualified of all my class rosters. And she never gave me the impression she was a snob. I'd spent a lot of time—and I do mean a lot—watching her when she was deeply engrossed in whatever she was doing. The woman was immeasurably kind, conscientious, and compassionate. It was also impossible to overlook how often the word young seemed to sneak into all my thoughts about her too.

My email pinged that a new message arrived, and my breath caught in my chest. It had been the same routine for the past two days every time that damn chime went off. I had switched the sound off so many times, only to give in and turn it back on to ensure I didn't miss a message while preoccupied.

Not that I had been getting any actual work done. I wanted to beat myself over the head with something big and heavy. I couldn't remember feeling so enthralled by a woman. Ever. When I tried to pinpoint what it was about this female specifically, I spent too long focusing on all her attributes and ended up in the private restroom across the hall with my dick in my fist.

Enough already!

When I opened the email program on the school-issued laptop, my heart rate doubled. The only new message in the incoming queue was finally from her.

Dear Dr. Chaplin,

I wanted to thank you again for taking the time to meet with me regarding the summer internship. After much consideration, I'm happy to accept the offer and look forward to receiving further instruction regarding the hours we will work, location, and so forth. You can respond to this email address, as I check it often. Also, my cellphone number is (925) 555-3038.

Kindly,

Maye L. Farsey

Calmly I closed the lid of the computer and sat back in my seat. With my index fingers steepled beneath my chin, I sat there for long minutes contemplating what I was getting myself into.

Maye L. Farsey. My imagination took off trying to think of perfect middle names that lone letter could represent. Was it an ordinary name like Lynn? Or something more creative like Luna? At this point in my teaching career, I'd seen so many unusual names, I could spend the rest of the day guessing and still not get it right.

Would the temptation of the woman be too great? I could lose my job and therefore, the last ten years of my life. I was being considered for tenure, a goal I had set for myself when first hired. Having a guaranteed contract with the university would take so much worry off my plate. Living in Los Angeles was unreasonably expensive, plus I had been supporting my mother in Nebraska since my father passed away three years ago. Counting on the annual cost of living increases the university offered with tenure would ensure I could stay in the area and continue doing what I loved: teaching and applying for grants on behalf of the school.

When I reminded myself of all the things I busted my ass for over the past decade, and all the responsibilities weighing me down, I felt like an immature boy for devoting so much time to crushing on a student. It wasn't simply amoral. It was career suicide. Ending my career would mean instant financial crisis, and I owed my mother and, frankly, myself, more than that sort of recklessness.

Those thoughts cemented a healthier mindset. Maye Farsey would complete the internship under my direction, and when the summer was over, our relationship would be nothing more than it currently was. I was a forty-year-old man, for Christ's sake. My hormones didn't dictate my actions when I was a younger man. They certainly wouldn't now either.

Just to remain on the safe side, I decided to respond to her via email. If I had to listen to that husky alto voice over the phone, I'd be trapped in my office again until my dick settled down.

Dear Ms. Farsey,

The internship program dictates you work alongside your mentor for at least fifteen hours each week. I've attached a copy of the university's requirements you should have received when applying. Please make yourself familiar with the expectations so we don't have to waste the valuable time we have together.

The first week we will meet in my business office on campus, but the location will potentially change as research becomes necessary. Please secure reliable transportation, as only one absence is acceptable. As you know from my classroom procedures, I do not tolerate tardiness. The same applies for this opportunity.

Our first session will start Wednesday morning at 8:00 a.m. Be prompt. A laptop, notebook, and writing implement will be necessary.

Sincerely,

Dr. Andrew Chaplin

Out of habit, I checked the message twice for errors and,

with a shaking hand, pressed Send.

Maybe if I could pinpoint what it was about this woman that had me so enthralled, I could stop the way my body was involuntarily responding. I had already given myself two mental lectures about the ridiculousness of the behavior but then sat daydreaming about her instead. What was next? Doodling her name on a scrap of paper in different combinations with my own?

I strode across the small office and yanked the old aluminum blind's cord to raise it out of the way. Maybe I just needed to get some fresh air circulating through the crowded space. As it stood currently, days had passed since she'd been here, and I still couldn't get that alluring fragrance of morning glories out of my nose.

Dust billowed from the sill as I threw open the ancient sliding window. The ledge looked like it hadn't been dusted all semester. Our school's janitorial staff had been on a labor strike for the past two months, so it had been at least that long. I'd have to bring a few cleaning supplies with me from home and clean up a bit before Wednesday.

Regardless of what I told myself about the motivation, my mother raised me better than to work or live in a filthy environment. The nagging voice in my mind that kept insisting I wanted to make a good impression on Maye could fuck off. I'd heard just about enough input from that nuisance at this point.

Possibly that was the way to conquer the guilt-and-excitement cocktail brewing within me. Ignore my conscience or voice of reason or whatever the hell it was that kept warning me I was getting in over my head. If I could shut that damn nag up for the summer, we'd all be in a more productive place. I couldn't go through the next couple of months second-guessing myself on every decision, every thought, and every word I spoke to the woman. I'd drive myself insane.

The next thirty-six hours were the longest of my life.

Even though I ended up cleaning my university office from top to bottom, it still looked cramped and shoddy. Hell! It was cramped and shoddy, and no amount of lipstick would change it from the pig it was.

The best outcome from the intense cleaning session was the room smelled heavily like bleach and pine oil. My nose actually tingled from the fumes, but not a whiff of her intoxicating fragrance could be detected.

My nosy office neighbor stopped in yesterday to see what the chemical odors were about, but it was really an excuse to take me off task. Ms. Donnio had occupied the space next to mine for the past school year, and without fail, she popped her pointy nose in my door to strike up an unwanted conversation every time we had common office hours.

One of my male colleagues insisted she was there to flirt after witnessing her predictable behavior, but I shut down his nonsense immediately. The gossip monster was a problematic presence on campus, and I'd rather do anything than get swept up in that sort of nonsense. I encouraged him to ask her out if he thought she was such a great catch, and his answer still rubbed me the wrong way.

"No," he'd laughed. "I mean, she'd be a great choice for you." Then another forced laugh. "Not me. She's not even close to my type."

"What would make you think she's my type, though?" Because honestly, she was the exact opposite of anyone I'd ever dated, but he didn't know anything about what I looked for in a woman. I wasn't in the habit of discussing my personal life with coworkers. Dating colleagues was just a recipe for disaster.

Something my father used to say ran through my mind. "You should never get your meal where you make your bread." It made me grin every time I thought of one of his funny little sayings, and he was full of them. "Pearls of wisdom," as he called them.

After straightening up one last time, I locked the door and headed to the parking lot. My car was one of a handful still there, and I took a deep lungful of fresh air while heading that way.

"Dr. Chaplin?" a female voice called from behind me when I was halfway across the lot. "Andrew?"

Great. Ms. Donnio was waving me down when I turned around, and there was no way to pretend I didn't hear her. I stuffed my hands in my pockets and waited for her to catch up. I'd see what she wanted and get on my way. I really just wanted to pick up some takeout and go home. I was exhausted from cleaning all day and needed a shower.

"Hey." She smiled, and instantly I was uncomfortable. "I— I didn't hear you leave." She thumbed back over her shoulder toward the building, as if I didn't know where I just left from. She shrugged and went on, "I— Umm...I thought maybe we could get dinner or something?"

At least, as she stood there stammering, she looked as out of place as I felt. Nothing about this pairing would be right.

"I appreciate the offer, but I'm really tired and just want to call it a day. My intern starts tomorrow," I explained and then added, "and you know how that goes." I rolled my eyes, acting as if this whole program were a burden.

"Oh, okay." She looked crestfallen, but I didn't care.

Maybe turning her down indirectly all year had been a mistake. At least she seemed to hear me when I was straightforward. "Maybe another time," she offered with a sliver of hope.

Since I was exhausted, I was a bit short-tempered. "No, I'm really not interested in you that way. I don't believe dating colleagues is a good idea. Ever."

What I wasn't about to tell her was that I tried that once. One time was all it took for me to lose my job at the private school I worked at. Harmlessly, I asked one of my coworkers to join me for a drink after work, and she couldn't keep her mouth quiet about the date. Within days, the board of directors called an emergency meeting to discuss my "lewd" behavior, as they dramatically labeled it, and I was given the nonchoice to resign quietly or be publicly made an example. The whole situation was bullshit, and I still resented the way it was handled. But I tried to leave it in the past with all the other things I regretted in my life.

Sleep proved to be an elusive creature that evening. I finally gave up and got up earlier than planned and went for a long run. Summer months were the best for predawn runs, and my nerves needed the chance to unwind before I got to my office. Even though I would've preferred more sleep, I was energized by the workout and opened the creaky door to my space with half a grin.

She'd be here within the hour, and just from that simple thought, my stomach tightened and my throat seemed to narrow.

"She's just like every other student," I kept repeating to myself, hoping to block any anxiousness. So far, it wasn't doing much good, but I had to keep something on a loop in there. Otherwise, thoughts and fantasies about my student would take over.

I wonder what her skin feels like.

I wonder if she smells like morning glories naturally or if it's a perfume she wears. Maybe it's a lotion, and that's why she always looks so silky smooth and buttery soft in all the best ways.

"Good morning," she said, and I nearly jumped out of my skin. Lost further in a fantasy about her than I cared to examine, I didn't even hear the door open.

"Oh, sorry," she said shyly without lifting her eyes to mine. "I didn't mean to surprise you. Isn't that the worst?" she asked with that stunning smile that promised a hundred other amusing thoughts were just waiting to be set free.

But we were here to work and learn, so I dug in. "You can set up your stuff on that side of the desk. I know it's cramped in here, but it should be workable for the time being. As I said in my email, we will likely move to the library in a week or two, depending on how quickly we can secure one of the private rooms."

Instantly my mind took off again, wanting so badly to list all the things I'd like to do to this stunning woman if given guaranteed privacy.

It was possible she'd dressed today specifically to make me crazy. Typically for class, she favored long flowing skirts and dresses that hid her body from everyone. Not today, though. Now I knew just what a crime against mankind those bohemian skirts were.

Today she went with a pair of straight-legged slacks and a simple button-front white blouse. Her blond hair that I routinely fantasized about touching, smelling, and pulling was usually pulled back from her face and secured in some sort of bun or braid. Again, not today. It cascaded down her back and brushed the waistband of her slacks. It was full and silky, and when I stood just close enough, I could smell that intoxicating scent I was obsessed with.

I made a mental note to do some online research on which hair product brands smelled like that bluish-purple flower.

No, Andrew. Stop this.

"So tell me before we get started, Ms. Farsey," I began, but she interrupted me.

"You can call me Maye. I mean, it's just the two of us working in here together, and it's going to be all summer. I don't mind if you drop the formality," she offered with a shy smile that rendered me speechless.

Why, though? I couldn't pinpoint it, but I attempted to respond—twice—and nothing came out. Christ, this behavior had to stop, or she wouldn't come back tomorrow. I was acting like an obsessed creeper, and it was ridiculous.

"Thank you," I finally said and had no idea what I was thanking her for exactly, but it was better than standing there just staring at the woman.

"And what would you like me to call you? Dr. Chaplin? Professor?"

Okay, this was comfortable territory. I'd had this discussion with my classes at the start of each new semester. If we dropped the title, it would feel way too personal.

"Yes, either of those is fine."

It took a few silent moments between us for me to remember what I had started saying. When I had my wits about me once again, I started over.

"So tell me why you're interested in grant writing as a career path."

"Isn't it obvious?" she asked without a hint of disrespect.

"To help people. I know universities, companies, individual students, public school districts—well, the list could go on and on, couldn't it?" She held my attention with her lively blue eyes while she spoke. "They all need financial help to some degree. I've read the statistics about how many grants go unawarded because applicants don't submit proper application packages."

She was rambling, and I was mesmerized.

"How sad is that? People want to help but can't because connecting the two parties has become so difficult."

She finally came up for air, and I was too lost in a dream world to respond.

Say something, you idiot.

After clearing my throat, I said, "That's an impressive answer. You've given it some thought." I said it as a statement, not a question that required her confirmation. It was obvious she found a field where her compassion, humanity, and intellect would be used to their fullest.

"Thank you," she nearly whispered, and I was baffled why such a capable woman would be so shy about receiving a compliment. With all her attributes, her self-esteem should enter every room before her. She could channel her passion into measurable success with a little direction.

I was definitely the man for the job.

CHAPTER FOUR

MAYE

Longest. Day. Ever. That's all my brain was capable of thinking as I drove home in stop-and-go traffic. Why was this city such a traffic nightmare all the time? And no matter which route you took, there were just certain hours of the day you had no other option than being part of it.

There was no way in hell I could do this three days a week. By the time I dropped my bag on my bed and kicked off my shoes, I wanted to face-plant directly into my covers. My sister wasn't home, so I had the room all to myself and began stripping off my clothes. Whether I had the energy for it or not, I needed a shower. The bleach and other cleaning products' fumes were so strong in the tiny little office all day, I swore even my hair smelled like Clorox.

There was a big, stupid grin across my entire face when I pictured Chaplin scrubbing that place until his fingertips were raw. I know with one hundred percent surety it wasn't that asphyxiating in there the day I went in for my interview. Well, noninterview, as it were.

While I was in the shower, one of my family members barged into the bathroom. Didn't knock, didn't ask if I'd be out soon, just came busting through the door like they were about to have an accident.

I knew it was Clemson before I peeked around the distorted glass enclosure to see who the rude intruder was.

"Clemmy, I'm in the shower. Do you mind?"

"Not at all. Carry on about your business," she answered through her infectious smile. It had always been her lethal weapon, and the girl knew how to brandish it when necessary.

"Get out. You can use the bathroom when I'm done," I insisted, my alto voice gaining volume with little effort.

"I just need to put my contacts in. I'm running late."

"Well, at least close the door. It's freezing in here with the draft from the hall," I complained just to have the last word. I had to feel like I had the upper hand in at least one conversation today. God knew that would never happen with Dr. Andrew Chaplin.

Clenching my jaw, I still felt all the frustrations of the day locked in that one joint. Pretty typical for me. But the man was such a freaking know-it-all, it was infuriating. Mostly because he was extremely intelligent and was right about everything. And he had no qualms about demonstrating it. Constantly. I knew this internship would be challenging, but it was looking like the most trying part of the opportunity would be interacting with him.

I really took a good look at him today while he was deeply engrossed in a task. He was classically good-looking in that every feature was beautifully symmetrical. His bone structure was divine—from his perfectly shaped and sized nose to his angular jaw. From what I could tell by seeing him in his suit and tie, he was also in excellent shape. I could appreciate a man who took care of himself.

But he needed to relax a bit. Okay, a lot. I'd hold out hope that as the weeks progressed, he would get more comfortable around me. It was the strangest combination. While he was incredibly smart and gifted at so many things, he seemed like a bumbling teenage boy when it came to personal conversation. Any attempt at small talk I made was met by awkward silence, a whole lot of body language that screamed *uncomfortable*, and finally snappy answers that shut down any hope of getting to know each other better on a personal level.

When I suggested we have lunch together, you would have thought I asked him to cosign a mortgage with me. He looked like he was involved in the most intense internal battle after I offered the idea—like he would've been more at ease making *Sophie's Choice*.

The serious guy didn't wear a wedding ring. After Shepperd's inquiry had me curious, I made it a point to check. There were no personal items in his office that I could see, either. Not a picture, house plant, or even a coffee mug with a clever quote.

As I dried off, I made up my mind to bring something personal for my half of the old desk. Maybe a picture of my family or a souvenir knick-knack just to liven up the place. If I spent too long in that drab space, I'd slip into a bout of depression. The one saving feature of the entire room was the windows. They were open part of the morning and let in tempting fragrances from the entire campus. I considered suggesting we move our operation outdoors when the bleachy smell finally turned my stomach.

But I knew I had to take baby steps with my rigid mentor. It was hard to picture Andrew Chaplin in the middle of a blanket on one of the grassy expanses around campus. The Wi-Fi was stable across the entire property, so he couldn't use that as an excuse when I did finally get up the courage to make the suggestion. Reading outdoors was one of my favorite pastimes. If I could overlay that joy on the tedium of researching material for this grant, the summer could actually be enjoyable.

I changed into pajamas right out of the shower, even though it was only dinner time. My plans for the evening were completely blown to hell when Professor Chaplin had handed me the biggest three-ring binder I'd ever seen when I was walking out the university door today. Now I had homework to do instead of spending the night out with my sisters.

Hannah had invited us over for one last girls' night before she gave birth, and I was really looking forward to spending time with my siblings. Even Shepperd was planning on going, but now that I had to stay home, she would more than likely cancel too.

Among all the other strange behaviors she'd developed over the past year, the most noticeable was how much she had pulled back from the family. We all spoke about it with regularity, but no one could come up with a reason why. She had confided in me once that she felt like everyone basically ganged up on her when we all assembled, and that she felt more comfortable when I was there too.

All we hoped and prayed for was that she hadn't gotten herself into anything dangerous or destructive. I kept telling myself the problem would eventually come to the surface and we'd all finally understand the changes in her mood and personality.

"Hello, daughter," my dad said after peeking his head through the doorway. "How did the first day go?"

"Hi, Daddy. It was fine. Exhausting, though. I'm not sure I'm qualified for what I'm doing, and I don't think my mentoring professor believes in my abilities either. Look at this enormous notebook he gave me to go through tonight." I pointed at the offending book on the foot of my bed.

He frowned. "I thought you were supposed to be going over to Hannah's place with your sisters?"

I sighed and let my shoulders drop down low. The disappointment was written all over my body before I said a word. "I was. Now I'll be here studying like it was three weeks ago and I was preparing for finals. I'm hoping this isn't going to be every evening," I said while scowling. My social life was already in the toilet. If I had to work every night when I really wanted free time, I'd turn into a very grumpy version of myself.

I didn't actually expect my dad to have a solution, so when he shrugged and said, "Well, I'll let you get to it," I wasn't surprised. "Your mom wanted me to let you know dinner will be ready in twenty minutes."

"Okay, thanks," I said with a forced smile. Maybe I could get away with eating in my room while I dug into the binder's contents. I closed the door behind him and flopped down on my bed. Scooting back against the headboard and some pillows, I started my task. It wasn't going to get done with me just bitching about it.

At some point, while reading the dry material, I dozed off. Instead of getting any measurable amount of reading done, I woke up to a dark, quiet room and a really stiff neck. The glasses I wore for reading were askew on my face from where I'd slumped over into the pillow stack.

Shepperd wasn't in her bed when I checked, so I wandered out to the kitchen. The clock on the oven said it was just after two in the morning. My mom left me a note on the island that she wrapped a plate for me and left it in the refrigerator. She was always thinking of us, no matter what she did. Honestly, though, I wished someone would've woken me up. Now, if I had any hope of making a dent in my assignment, I'd be up for the rest of the day.

With a plate of warmed-up pasta, I quietly crept back to my room. The food smelled heavenly, and my stomach rumbled, knowing it would soon be full and happy. I was so nervous around Dr. Chaplin that I barely ate lunch. My imagination toyed with me much of the day, and I kept feeling like the man was carefully studying me when he thought I was too deeply engrossed in my tasks to pay attention to what he was doing. When I lifted my focus from whatever I was doing and looked across the desk, he'd quickly busy himself with something. After the fourth time catching him staring at me, I was convinced it wasn't my imagination.

So the self-doubt set in. Why was he watching me so closely? Did he not think I could handle the simple tasks he gave me? I hoped it was just us getting to know each other and that he'd realize he could give me more important things to do and trust they'd be done properly. If the babysitting feeling was still there after week two, I decided I'd have a conversation with him.

The grant we were applying for first had a very simple list of requirements. I had offered to work on the cover letter, but he said no. The experienced teacher explained he always did the cover letter last so it would read more like a conclusion or synopsis rather than an introduction.

After considering his explanation for a few minutes, the only answer I could come up with was, "Okay."

Trying not to feel affronted, I waited for the task assignment he thought I could handle, and, well...it never came. If I were expected to simply shadow him for the next ten weeks, I'd go batty. I needed to be productive. I learned much faster by doing, and if it came down to it, he and I would have that discussion as well.

Now I had a very full stomach, and looking through the binder he sent me home with was putting me to sleep faster than a sci-fi movie. The more I read, the more bored and frustrated I felt. There was nothing of value in the entire notebook. It was a detailed outline of the very basics in applying for a grant. I'd studied this material in my second year.

I slapped the vinyl cover shut and tossed it to the foot of my bed. Apparently, with a little more force than I thought, because it slid right off the mattress and hit the floor with a thunk. When I got out from under the covers to retrieve the damn thing, I noticed several pages were sticking out and the front cover had broken at the spine. I could replace the damaged pages by copying the originals and swapping them out. But that left the bigger problem.

I didn't have a four-inch three-ring binder just lying around to swap the stuff into. Who would? I could just imagine the lecture I was in for about disrespecting his property or some nonsense like that. It was an accident! Accidents happen all the time.

This was ridiculous. It was approaching three in the morning, and I was getting myself near hysterical over torn pages and a damaged notebook. Why did this man have me so on edge? If I couldn't find my footing where he was concerned, I'd have to drop the internship. I didn't want to spend my summer tied up in knots over a man I couldn't stand.

Hell, I just dumped my boyfriend for the same reason.

But if I gave up on the internship, any hopes of being accepted into the master's degree program or being able to pay for it would fly right out the window. My parents agreed to cover four-year programs for all of us if we chose that route, but they also said we were on our own for postgraduate studies.

Okay. Okay. I needed to calm the hell down. My anxiety was nothing like our sister Hannah's. Thank God. I usually could get a grip on my physical state before it got out of hand.

Lots of inner dialogue, lots of self-coaching about regulating my breathing. See? There was nothing wrong here. That professor was just another person. Just another man. He didn't really have some sort of weird spell cast over me that made me want to please him beyond reason. He wasn't really as attractive as I'd been daydreaming about in the shower. He wasn't really staring at me constantly.

All in my overactive imagination. I took another deep breath and blew it out through pressed lips. The air made a little whistle on the exhale, and I was thankful Shep wasn't home to have witnessed that near meltdown. I decided to put the homework to the side and get some quality sleep. That nap I had earlier in the evening could carry me through the day if it had to, but if I wanted to be firing on all cylinders, I needed some deep sleep. I set my alarm for five thirty and turned out the lights. Hopefully Shepperd was out for the night and wouldn't come busting through the door at any moment.

But there was no escaping him, even in my dreams. Although the version of the man I had conjured in sleep was much more delightful. Much more engaging. And, heaven help me, much more appealing. Of course, we were back in that damn shoe-box-sized office, although in my dream, he had me spread out on that old wooden desk we were sharing and was looking up at me from between my legs. His eyes were so dark with lust, they looked black. As I arched into the climax he so masterfully brought me to, my alarm sounded, and the whole fantasy *poofed* out of existence.

What the hell was going on? I was not hot for Professor Chaplin. No way. I didn't need all kinds of confusing hormone-fueled thoughts complicating an already crappy situation. I couldn't deny the facts of my physical state, though. That dream was so damn vivid and good, I was still shaking from the orgasm. No point in beating myself up over it though and wrecking the high and consequential peace I always felt after getting off.

So I lay there a few more minutes and enjoyed the sensations coursing through my body. God, it had been too long since I had this feeling. Honestly, Joel was a terrible lover. It wasn't that he was selfish. Quite the opposite. He tried too hard to please me. In the end, it basically came down to I just wasn't into him. I trusted my heart and my head on the fact that you shouldn't have to try when you met *your* person. Everything was supposed to fall into place and just be right naturally. With Joel, it just wasn't right. It was that simple.

Time to get up, though, so off to the shower I trudged. This one was solely to wake up so I was at least functioning. If I could get out of the house with enough time, I'd hit the coffee shop on campus and get a caffeine boost.

Shepperd still wasn't home, and it didn't dawn on me until I stood on the long driveway helplessly staring at the spot our shared car was normally parked. How the hell was I going to get to school if she didn't pull in within the next few minutes? I was going to chew her a big fat new ass for this.

Professor Chaplin made it explicitly clear that he didn't tolerate bullshit reasons for being late or not showing up. I whipped out my phone and feverishly scrolled through my apps to call for a ride. I barely had enough money to buy a cup of coffee, so how the hell would I pay for a ride to school?

Calling any of my other sisters for help was out of the question too. Hannah lived in Malibu. By the time she got up and got to Brentwood, it would be lunchtime. Agatha was as irresponsible as Shepperd. Yes, she was doing so much better with that husband of hers on board, but I wouldn't ask her to bail me out of a jam unless I had no other choice.

Okay, I needed to calm down. I was standing in our driveway trying to make sense of the hire-a-ride app on my phone, and my hand was shaking so badly I could barely see the instructions. I mashed a few prompts on the display, and thank God! Toby was only two minutes away in a sensible red Nissan.

Thank you, Toby.

I'd figure out how poor Toby was actually going to be paid for his service on my ride to campus. I knew if I got in a serious bind—like I would definitely classify this as—my folks would slide me some money until I found a way to earn some myself and pay them back.

I needed a job. Then I could buy my own car and wouldn't have to be in this situation ever again. But even if I worked full-time all summer, I still wouldn't have enough for something road worthy. Everything was so damn expensive in Southern California. Well, everywhere, really.

My ride stopped at the end of the driveway, and I hustled to him. I slid into the back seat, slightly winded from the freak-out and the jog down to meet the car. Toby was a nice enough guy, even if he looked in the rearview mirror more than he did through the windshield. We actually plowed through a red light at a thankfully empty intersection because he was more concerned with my plans for the day than getting us to school safely.

"Oops, missed that one." He laughed and looked back at me again.

"Please keep your eyes on the road. I need to get there alive," I said once my stomach dropped back to its rightful place from where it had lodged in my throat.

"Sorry. Sorry. I'm an excellent driver, honest. It's just that..." He paused and looked at the navigation display on the dash.

Please don't ask me out. Please don't ask me out.

"It's just, I mean, you're really hot." He laughed a very uncomfortable-sounding laugh. "But you know that, right? I mean, shit...look at you, right? I bet you get asked out all the time. Do you have a boyfriend?"

Looking down at my phone, I tried to pretend I didn't hear him. When he repeated his ridiculous question, I looked up with a huff.

"No. I don't have a boyfriend. And thank you for the compliment. That's very kind of you," I said and faked a quick smile.

"Oh, I totally mean it too. So..." He paused for a long moment, and I dreaded what he was going to say next. "If you don't have a boyfriend..." Another long pause, and I considered bailing out the back door of the moving car. "You wanna go out sometime? This is a little awkward. I don't usually do this with my passengers. Really."

Christ. At least he had the sense to look sheepish after all that.

"No. Thank you, though," I said without looking up and decided to just leave it there. I didn't owe this stranger an explanation or a reason why I didn't want to go on a date with him. Hopefully the silence that ballooned between us in the small car would make him feel uncomfortable enough to forgo ever pulling that stunt again.

There. That was my good deed for the day. I did womankind a favor by gently teaching this clueless boy a lesson. Took one for the team and all that. The silly thought made me grin while I checked my email, and Toby must have caught the change of expression in the rearview.

"Ooooh, you're thinking about it, aren't you?" he exclaimed excitedly.

When I met his eyes in the rectangular mirror, I gave him the most incredulous look I could. "No, I'm not."

Fortunately, the ride was quicker than normal. Thank you, traffic gods, for gifting me that small grace. No way could I get coffee, though, since I drained my account paying Toby's fare. I'd have to be fine without the java boost. I walked through the door of Professor Chaplin's stuffy office with one minute to spare. According to my phone, anyway.

"I specifically said don't be late," he said without looking up from his laptop.

"I have a minute to spare," I said before thinking better of it.

Well, that made him instantly raise his eyes from his computer and sit back in his chair. When he whipped his glasses off his nose, I felt a bit of panic swell in my empty stomach.

Slowly, I raised my phone and showed him the display that read 7:59 a.m.

Without another word, he replaced his glasses and waved his hand toward my half of the desk. I took that to mean I should sit, so I cautiously lowered myself into the chair. That's when I noticed there was a new seat on my side of the desk.

Yesterday I sat in the same stiff, wooden chair I sat in for my noninterview. The furniture was likely older than me. Today, however, there was a very modern chair. It was the type you'd see at any office supply megastore, and it was incredibly comfortable. After wiggling my bottom deeper into the cushiony seat, I looked up to find him studying me intently.

"Thank you," I said, and my normally confident, strong voice sounded shy and feminine. What the hell was going on here? Over a freaking chair?

But the thing was, I had a feeling this man didn't go out of his way for anyone. I hadn't complained about that awful chair yesterday, but he must have known it was uncomfortable. He went the extra mile to make things a little nicer for me, and those were the kind of things that mattered to me. It didn't have to be a grand, over-the-top gesture or item. It was the little things that counted.

But instead of responding like a person usually would, he just redirected his focus with a quick nod like it never happened. Man, this guy was confusing. So I chose to also not make a big deal out of it and got out my laptop and set up my desk for the day ahead. When I felt his eyes on me again, I looked up and caught him completely staring at me this time.

So I held his gaze and waited. If he had something to say, he was either having second thoughts about saying it or was content just studying me like I was the project.

I finally caved and said, "Is there something wrong?"

"I don't think so. Do *you* have something you need to address?"

I slowly shook my head but never looked away. This guy

wasn't going to intimidate me with his directness. I rather preferred it, honestly. Most people my age didn't have the confidence to be so forthright. Maybe it was one of the things I found attractive about the man.

Wait a minute. One of the things? Was there a list now?

"Today I want you to research these four websites." He slid a piece of paper closer to me on the desk, then stood and rounded to my side. I studied his hand while it rested on top of the white sheet. His skin was darker than mine, and against the snowy comparison of the paper, the tone looked even richer than I had registered before. Long, straight fingers with impeccably clean, blunt nails spanned the paper from left to right. The man definitely took care of himself, and I inhaled a slow breath to focus.

Websites. Look at the web addresses.

After finally nodding, I asked, "What would you like me to look for on these websites?" When I looked closer, I was familiar with three of the four. These were commonly used sites that databased available grants, had documentation on the funding sources, and detailed the requirements to apply for the available money listed.

"Oh, okay," I said more to myself than him.

"You're familiar?" he asked with a raised brow.

"Yes, with these three," I replied while pointing to the list. "This fourth one is new to me, but I'll take a look and get familiar with it," I said while angling back toward my computer.

When he didn't go back to his side of the desk, I looked up at him. Instantly that damn dream I had flooded my mind with naughty images, and I felt my face flush. I knew from living my whole life with the terrible problem, my complexion was beet red. Additionally, the embarrassment of knowing it was happening made the blushing exponentially worse. Nervously, I looked up again to find him studying my every move.

"Are you unwell? Your face is suddenly very flushed. Is it too hot in here for you?" He asked all three questions in a flurry and rushed to the window to let in some cool morning air. Even if I weren't overheating because of anxiety and embarrassment, I wouldn't stop him from his task. If I spent another day breathing the bleachy fumes that still lingered in the room, I'd have a migraine for sure.

"Yes, please. If you don't mind. I think some fresh air in here would be lovely. Can I help?" I asked out of habit while standing. My parents raised us with very good manners. Also, it was my natural inclination to offer help to anyone who was doing something while I was not.

"I'll do it. These old things are stiff. Some of them haven't been opened in decades, I'd venture to say," he explained, and I was speechless. Even though the subject matter was ridiculous, it was the most personable Dr. Chaplin had been since the day I met him in class. The muscles in his back strained against his tailored button-down while he really leaned into prying open the sash. I was transfixed by the site.

After successfully opening two of the four windows, he returned to his seat across from me. "Better?" he asked. "Your color has returned to normal," he observed quietly but immediately looked down and busied himself with something in his desk drawer.

Interesting. Maybe he was regretting letting his guard down just then. If I was reading his body language correctly, he was unsure of himself and not happy in that space.

I didn't want to antagonize the guy, so I set about my task. But then realized he still hadn't told me exactly what he wanted me to do on each web page. I didn't need to familiarize myself with them on his time. I already knew my way around all but one. That's where I started and figured I'd wait for him to further instruct me. After about twenty minutes of surfing around the page, I explored all I could without a purpose.

"Dr. Chaplin?" I said before looking up. Once again, his dark-brown eyes were already assessing me when I did.

"Yes, Ms. Farsey?" he said with no inflection in his tone. Was all of this boring to him and he was just going along with the program to make some summer cash? I knew a lot of professors took on interns as a way to supplement their incomes between semesters. Maybe that's what was going on here? He didn't want to be here any more than I did. It was just what we had to do to get what we wanted. Lucky me would be the target of his resentment for the next three months.

"Please call me Maye. It feels like we're still in class when you're so formal," I suggested again with a kind, genuine smile. His blank stare made me regret the suggestion immediately. Instead of continuing down that uncomfortable path, I asked, "What do you want me to look for?" I sputtered. "On these websites?"

"You said you were familiar with them," he began, and I cut him off.

"I am, but there are many things I could be doing instead of just surfing. Are you looking for specific grants for research projects done by a university, for example? Or were you wanting to look at a narrowed-down field, like psychology in this case?"

I waited for him to answer, but he just looked annoyed.

I don't know if it was the way my morning started, my frustration with my sister, my annoyance with Toby, or what possessed me in the next moment, but I threw my hands up and stood abruptly.

Not taking his attention off me for a second, he saw my little tantrum and shifted in his chair.

"Sit down," he said firmly, and his dark, commanding voice stole my free will. I plopped angrily back into the chair, and the force of my weight hitting the seat made it roll back about two feet from the desk. In that brief moment, he was on his feet and occupied the space between me and the desk.

My eyes were just about crotch level as he crowded into my personal space, and my heart beat a crazy staccato.

He perched on the edge of the desk and leaned back with his arms behind him. "Do we have a problem this morning, Ms. Farsey?"

"Maye," I muttered under my breath. He was looming so close there was no way he didn't hear me.

I couldn't make eye contact with him, though. If he hadn't caged me in, I would've made some sort of excuse and hurried out of the room. And my God, how had I not noticed how intoxicating he smelled before that moment? The fresh breeze made the scents I gravitated toward in a men's cologne swirl between us in the crowded room. It was as though he knew my preferences and made a one-of-a-kind cocktail to drive me insane.

Bravely I let my eyes crawl up his abdomen to his firm chest. Praise to the man's tailor, because his white dress shirt showed every hill and valley of his physique on that side too. I continued my visual trip to his taut neck and angular jaw. His dark eyes reeled me in like helpless prey.

He studied me wordlessly, and I grew bolder and held his gaze for a long moment. Until his lips parted ever so slightly, and he sneaked his tongue out to wet the inviting pair. The sight made me audibly gasp, and I froze with a heady combination of arousal and fear. Thankfully the groan that was trying desperately to claw its way out got caught in my throat or I would've died of embarrassment right where I sat.

"Maye," he finally repeated. He said my name with careful enunciation like he was caressing me intimately with the sound. My heart rate picked up a little more from just hearing him say my name. While I continued the staring contest with him, I imagined him saying my name while he worshiped my body between pronouncing it in different ways. He made the simple name sound sexy and sinful, and I had to shift in my seat.

This couldn't be good. There was no way in hell I should be getting aroused by my professor. A man who had to be twenty years older than I was. We had nearly three months ahead of us in this tiny space. Alone. But there was an electricity flowing between us today that was undeniable. I wouldn't dare mention the sensation I was feeling in case it was my lonely libido crying for stimulation.

Yes, that had to be it. It was the only reasonable explanation. I gave my head an abrupt shake and cleared my throat. The combination of gestures snapped him out of the same spell I had been under, and he stood to his full height. Finally, he moved to his side of the desk.

I focused on my computer monitor, though I couldn't see a single letter or image on the display. My attention was on him shifting around in his chair until he finally sat comfortably.

I wouldn't even let my mind wander to the reasons why sitting was suddenly uncomfortable for the guy. Definitely not going there.

CHAPTER FIVE

ANDREW

Idiot. What the hell did I just do? There was no way this arrangement could work. She was too much of a temptress. And the craziest part of it all? She didn't even know what she was doing to me. Well, she might have had a solid clue after that. That increased her allure, though. I never cared for the dramatic type. Or high-maintenance women, as they usually proudly proclaimed themselves. But apparently the quiet, intelligent, humble young ladies tripped my trigger just fine.

And let's sit with the word young for a moment.

Young as in twenty years younger than me. Young as in born my sophomore year of college, for Christ's sake. While I shifted around in my chair, trying to regain normal circulation to my dick and balls, I made a decision. I'd have to find a loophole that would end this internship without hurting her chances in the master's program. I probably couldn't do much about the tuition grant that came along with the internship, but she lived in Brentwood. Her folks couldn't be hurting too bad financially.

I chanced another look over at the siren. Her glazed-over stare gave away that she was struggling with what had just happened too, but I assumed for different reasons altogether. She probably thought I was a lecherous older man after I pulled that unthinkable stunt—wedging my body between the desk and her. If I had thought that through for even five seconds, I would've never done it. But instead, I used all my mental strength to act like a domineering animal.

"Maybe we should go to the library today?" Maye suggested quietly.

It wasn't a bad idea, but what if there were other professors or students there? The campus library was one of the few buildings that stayed open between semesters and was also open for the general public to use.

"I've scheduled time for that next week." I didn't miss her disappointed reaction, so I added, "That was the soonest I could secure one of the private rooms so we won't be disturbed."

"Oh, okay," she said without looking up. Why did I have such a hard time reading this woman? I kept telling myself it was her age, but that didn't hold much credibility. I dealt with people her age day in and day out. I was used to the generation's slang and body language.

The real issue was Maye Farsey wasn't like most people her age.

She had a quiet reservation about her, while at the same time she radiated a confidence that was like catnip to me. But those two traits were often contradictory, and I was right back to square one of my confusion.

Time to focus on why we were here. Maybe if I overloaded her with work, she'd quit the program on her own, and I wouldn't have to be the bad guy. Hmm, the idea had potential. I must have been lost in the thought longer than I realized because her next comment caught me off guard.

"What are you smiling about?" She shrugged when I focused on her instead of staying lost in my own mind. "Just curious."

"Oh, I didn't realize... I was, just...well, never mind. Getting back to your questions from before, let's discuss what I'd like you to research on those four websites, and then you can get busy, yes?"

I gave myself a mental pat on the back for reestablishing some boundaries. If I didn't keep pep-talking myself for staying professional, I'd probably slip up again. I didn't know the woman well, but I could fairly predict she wouldn't tolerate too many incidents like the one we just shared.

Without waiting for her to agree or disagree with the plan, I rounded the desk again and leaned over her shoulder. Tapping the first website address, I instructed, "This site is typically the most current. Or at least that has been my experience. If you find an opportunity there, you will likely see it pop up on the others within the week. For some reason, though, this is everyone's first choice when listing."

"Sponsors," she added quietly.

"Pardon?"

"I think it's because of the number of sponsors they've secured. Look at the landing page alone. One, two," she counted off as she pointed at different ads scattered around the screen. "Sponsors drive traffic to websites."

"That's very observant," I commented. "I think you're probably right."

Just one slight nod for the compliment, and then she opened a small notebook she pulled from her bag. With pen in hand, she waited for me to continue explaining what I wanted.

We spoke about her task for a few more minutes before I took my own seat again. I had a long list of unopened emails to tend to while she tapped away on her laptop. We worked in silence for about an hour, and I was thankful she hadn't caught me staring at her but once. She was very focused on her work, and I on her.

Finally, I excused myself to use the restroom to get some much-needed space between us. The fresh morning air breezing through the open windows mixed with Maye's subtle perfume, and her scent was crawling all over me like eighteen sets of fingertips. Light and floral, her perfume had me fantasizing about fucking her out in nature somewhere. If I didn't get some sort of distraction quick, I was in danger of tackling her on our shared desk.

Like a bumbling schoolboy, I nearly tripped over my own feet as I hurried from the office and out into the hall. I got about halfway down the corridor when my nosy hallway neighbor, Ms. Donnio, popped her head out of her office.

"Ooooh, hello, Andrew. I was hoping it was you out here. On a break?" She smiled coyly, and any arousal troubling me from my intern vanished immediately.

"No, on an errand at the moment. Can't chat now," I said hurriedly and never stopped walking. My goal was the stairwell door at the end of the corridor, and I focused on it while shouting back over my shoulder.

"Want some company?" the clueless woman offered as she rushed toward me.

I stopped and pivoted on her. Damn, the woman could hustle for the heel height she was sporting. In that brief pause it took me to think that random thought, she closed the remaining distance between us.

"Really, Ms. Donnio, I'm just running across campus. I'm sure you'd rather..."

She grabbed my forearm with an impressive grip and said,

"Don't be silly, Andrew. I'd love to come along."

Firstly, I thought while looking pointedly at her fingers clutching my forearm, I didn't invite her. She invited herself. Secondly, there was only one woman I wanted to spend time with at the moment. She was both forbidden and too young, and was the exact person I was escaping with this fabricated errand. But I wasn't about to say any of those things to this one.

As much as I hated being a dick, contrary to what everyone thought about me, it was obviously the only tact that would get through to my pushy colleague.

"Listen, I really wanted to be alone. I'm sorry, but I don't want company."

She lifted her hand off my body—finally—and her demeanor turned on a pinpoint. I'd hurt her feelings, and she was about to be a very poor sport about it. I'd seen this behavior one hundred times in other women, so I braced for the impact of whatever she was about to spew.

"Are you gay?" she blurted, as if it were a reasonable conclusion to draw. As if it were her business in the first place.

"Pardon?" I asked without thinking but then quickly held up my flat palm between us. "No, never mind. I'm not going to even address that ignorance." Shaking my head, I couldn't form an acceptable follow-up or farewell, so I simply turned and walked away. Down the flights of stairs to the ground floor and out into the beautiful summer day.

There was no other goal at the crux of this game plan, just putting distance between me and the alluring creature in my office. Now that I stood in front of the office building, I had no idea what to do.

I wasn't the kind of man who lazed about. Leisure time, if I ever had any, was usually spent grading papers or doing chores around my house that had been neglected throughout the week. Some semesters, if I felt ambitious, I would teach a continuing education class at night. The extra money was always nice, plus the board of directors took those sorts of things into consideration when deciding who would be granted tenure.

After completing two slow and mindless laps around the building, I decided I'd calmed down enough to go back inside to my office. It would be lunch break soon, and I'd get another spell of time away from her. How the hell was I going to survive the entire summer this way? Maybe I needed to swipe right on one of the women who kept messaging me on that tedious dating app I joined and set something up for the weekend. If I could blow off some sexual steam with a casual hookup, I wouldn't be in a constant state of arousal.

Yeah, right. Keep telling yourself that, Chaplin.

But just thinking of going through that awful process of taking someone out, pretending to be interested, spending money I didn't have, just in hopes of getting laid... Yeah, it just wasn't my scene. I'd never been good at one-night stands anyway, and now that Maye was occupying so much of my headspace, it would be even worse.

When I opened the door to my office, she was gone. A wave of panic instantly swelled in my stomach and rose up into my chest. The compressing feeling made it difficult to breathe, and I burst back out into the hall. She wasn't wandering around out there either, but of course, when I caught my breath again and gave it some thought, I already knew that. I would've seen her when I walked the exact path I was blindly searching now.

"Get a fucking grip, Andrew," I muttered to myself and went back inside and sank down into my chair. Her laptop was still on the desk, open to the website she'd been searching when I bailed out like a passenger aboard a sinking ship. The screen was still active, so she hadn't been gone long—or long enough for it to switch into sleep mode, at least. Her canvas tote that seemed to be a uniform staple for girls her age wasn't slung over the back of her chair, though, and the panic fought to gain space in my gut again.

"No," I said to the empty room. "Stop." There had to be a logical explanation as to her whereabouts. She wouldn't leave her computer behind if she'd left for the day. One thing was clear—I really needed to get my shit together around this student. No more personal space invasions, no more daydreams—or night dreams, for that matter. We had to maintain a professional teacher-student relationship and nothing more.

The sound of the old doorknob turning caught my attention, and I shot my gaze to the entrance. She came floating in and gave me a soft smile. As she slung her bag over the back of her chair, she said, "Sorry. I wasn't sure how long you'd be, and I really needed a bio break."

I waved my hand like swatting away a gnat. "It's fine. Of course, you should use the facilities as necessary. You don't need to wait for permission, Maye."

Her eyes widened when I said her name. Even I could hear how my voice had dropped in range as I formed the sound. Definitely unintentional but undeniable as well. My body knew what it wanted, and it was betraying me in order to interest her.

Choosing to press on and ignore the moment, I asked, "How's it going there? Have you found anything promising?"

She sat down and bounced a little with excitement. "Yes,

actually. I found a few things that look doable. The timeline on the largest is a little tight, but I think if we put in a little bit of overtime, we could have our package ready for submission in time."

I was absorbing her excitement as she spoke and found myself sitting forward on the edge of my chair and watching the delicate skin on her neck stretch and flex as she spoke.

What I wouldn't give to run my nose along the graceful curve of her throat. Lick her milky skin that looked so silky smooth. She was a stunning woman. Her youth and current vibrant passion for her work made her even more beautiful.

I was going to hell for this. That's all there was to it. Every time I was reminded how young she was, I could almost hear Satan chuckling in my subconscious. It was like the bastard brought this enticing female my way just to test my resolve.

If she gave me one hint of a green light that she was feeling the way I was, I'd have her on her back quicker than either of us could calculate. My body would take over at that point, and I'd be helpless to do anything other than go along for the ride. And fuck me, what a life-altering ride it would be.

Perfect. Now I had an erection—again. Maye had been chattering the entire time I was lost in my dirty thoughts and was now pointing at her monitor. Finally, I swam to the surface of the lust pool I'd been deep diving in long enough to hear her say, "Come look at this," while she pointed emphatically at her monitor.

Mud. Seaweed. Ms. Donnio. I thought of as many gross things as I could to kill my hard-on so I could stand up and not be embarrassed.

I stammered for a plausible excuse. "Actually, will you send me a link to the page you're on? That way I'll have it in my

history as well in case I work on the application from home."
It was a reasonable enough explanation, regardless of it being
complete bullshit.

Apparently it was good enough, though. "Oh, great idea. I
was thinking while you were out getting some air"—she looked
up sheepishly—"or whatever you were doing..." She waved her
hand as though she were swiping the complicated thought out
of the way. "I didn't mean to be presumptuous."

I didn't respond with words. Just gave her a curt nod to
continue. If the elephant in this room got any bigger, we'd have
to move to a new location to work.

"Anyway, I was thinking maybe we should outline who's
working on what so we don't double our efforts and waste
precious time. What do you think?"

Finally able to stand without having a tent in my slacks,
I went to her side of our shared desk. Quickly scanning over
the grant she had on her screen, I saw she had stumbled upon
a golden opportunity. If we applied for this money and were
awarded it, I'd undoubtedly secure tenure and she'd earn that
scholarship.

I looked at her for a long moment. "This is amazing. You
did a great job here," I praised while tapping her screen. "This
is exactly what the department needs, and if we could secure
this one grant, we wouldn't need the other two I had in mind."

Pride radiated from my student, and her happiness
warmed my gut. One of the highlights of teaching had always
been creating successful students. The feeling I had at that
moment reminded me why I suffered through the bureaucratic
bullshit from the university, the piss-poor attitudes from most
of the student body, and the long uncompensated hours I put
in on the side. Seeing her realize success was a reward of its

own. I could just imagine how contagious it would be if we were awarded the grant.

"Maybe... Oh, I don't know," she said first with excitement and then immediately second-guessed herself.

"Maye?" I captured her attention with her name.

"Hmm?"

"I want you to stop doubting yourself. I want to hear your ideas as much as I expect you to listen to mine. All right?"

She nodded, swallowed roughly, and voiced her thought. "Well, I was thinking, maybe we should still apply for at least one of the others in case this one doesn't work out. Like a safety net, you know?"

"That's a fair point. And I appreciate your caution," I said and watched my positive feedback light her up from within. "Trust your intuition. You're a very smart woman. You can rely on your intelligence more than a lot of your peers." And I meant every word I said.

"Thank you, Dr. Chaplin. I appreciate you saying those things," she said through a devastating smile. If possible, she was even more radiant when doing something she was excited about.

I sat down in my own chair and clicked on the link she'd sent me.

From the other side of the desk, she asked, "So what do you think about making a list of tasks and then dividing them up? That's how my sisters and I get the chores done around our house. That way we stay focused."

While she was talking, I navigated to a file I created years ago. It was exactly what she was talking about, and admittedly, I was anxious to show her that we shared a similar brainstorm.

"I'm air-dropping you a document. You'll probably want

to set my contact to autoaccept to make it easier for us to share files back and forth." My own excitement was building off hers.

I listened to the different sounds coming from her laptop as she received the file. After a few clicks, I watched her bright-blue eyes dart from left to right. Left to right again and again as she looked at the outline of tasks.

"Yes, this is exactly what I was thinking." Her face went from excited to serious. I couldn't anticipate what she was about to say. "Thank you for letting me be part of the process. It makes a big difference when I feel like I'm appreciated for what I can bring to the table instead of being stuffed into the corner and just called on when needed for something you don't want to do yourself."

I was shocked. And deflated more than I had words for. "Maye," I said, just to feel her name in my mouth. "Have I made you feel that way?"

Immediately she tried to smooth over my disappointment. "No, not completely. And don't get me wrong, I will totally do what I'm assigned to do. I just feel like I stay more engaged when I'm seen." She looked down to where she was twisting her fingers in her lap. "I'm not sure if any of that made sense?"

Her last thought was posed as a question, and to be honest, I wasn't one hundred percent clear on what she meant, but I thought it made a degree of sense.

"I think I understand," I said, and she nodded, seemingly satisfied that I at least acknowledged her comment. So I continued. "You were chosen for this internship based on your skill set, interest level, and performance in class. Those were the standards used in making the decision."

"Thank you."

"That being said, I can only hope that one reason for you

accepting the position was to learn from my expertise. My experience." She looked like she wanted to say something, so I paused there.

"It is. That's exactly how I see this opportunity too."

"Then you have to be willing to take direction, even if in the moment you don't understand why I'm asking you to do something. You can rest assured that I have no interest in wasting your time on silly tasks." Then I added under my breath, "Or mine, for that matter."

There was a certain level of admiration and appreciation for her bravery to voice her concerns. At the same time, she needed to understand there was only room enough for one cook in this kitchen. Me.

After checking the time, I decided we had pretty much lost our momentum with our research, so it was a good time to break for lunch. "Let's take an hour for lunch and be back here"—I pointedly looked at my watch—"at 12:45 p.m. There's still a lot to get through today to stay on schedule."

"No worries. I just need about twenty minutes to scarf down the sandwich I brought, and I'll be ready to get back to it," she said brightly and pulled a brown paper bag from her tote.

Christ, that thing was like a bag of magic tricks. How the hell much fit in that one fabric sack?

Fascinated by everything she did, I stood and stared while she set up a little dining spot on her desk. I must have stayed riveted to the same spot too long, because she finally looked up from what she was doing.

"You're staying here?" I asked and winced when I registered how rude I sounded.

"Do you need me to leave?" she asked with a reasonable

amount of confusion. Before I could excuse my rudeness, she hastily began packing her food back up.

Then I did the dumbest thing to date with the young woman. I reached out and touched her arm to still her activity. The moment my hand felt the buttery soft skin on the inside of her forearm, I gasped. Gasped so loudly, she jerked her arm away and stood.

"Sorry," I stammered. "Really, I am. I had no right to do that." I swallowed the anxiety choking my air off.

She watched my every uncomfortable move with the attention of a scientist studying a specimen. She had to think I'd lost my damn mind.

It was possible I had.

CHAPTER SIX

MAYE

Up until that moment, I had convinced myself I was imagining some sort of electricity between us. I mean really, what was I basing it on? A bunch of schoolgirl-style mooning over her obviously incredibly handsome and intelligent proctor?

And then he touched me.

And I knew it wasn't my overactive imagination, or my lonely libido, or whatever other excuse I had made to explain away what I thought was building between us. When Professor Chaplin yanked his hand back from my bare skin, I knew he felt it too. The panicked look on his face punctuated the theory.

"It's fine," I said in nearly a whisper. Neither of us could miss how throaty my voice sounded when I vocalized the assurance. I knew it was the exact same way it sounded when I was aroused.

Heat flooded my chest, neck, and face. I felt the blood rushing to bloat every tiny capillary responsible for the reaction. The blushing was a dead giveaway I was way too intrigued by the meaningless gesture. When I finally cleared my thoughts enough to look away, it was too late. He was observing me like I was a zoo animal, and my instinct was to bolt.

I dropped my untouched sandwich onto the napkin I'd

so carefully laid out on the desk and rushed for the door. But Chaplin predicted my plan and blocked the door with his incredible body before I could flee.

"Don't go," he said, breathing through flared nostrils. My stare traveled from his pecs, up past his throat and prominent Adam's apple, to his lush, parted lips. Finally, I forced myself to look into his dark stare and tried to read what was happening.

Once, twice, three times I tried to speak and couldn't rationalize a single statement that fit the moment. What did I think I would say to this mesmerizing man?

Take me home with you ran out in front of the others as the choice that best expressed what I was feeling. The more sensible side of my brain put a stop to that—*thankfully*. The man was my teacher. My teacher who was old enough to know better than to bed his student.

But my body was having a riotous tantrum at the moment. My heartbeat thundered in my ears, so even if he did say something, I didn't think I'd hear him. But he stood frozen in that spot. Not speaking. Not moving. Hell, was he breathing?

"I'm sorry," I finally croaked, and the sound seemed to shake him from whatever stupor he was in. He shook his head ever so slightly and opened his mouth to reply. But just as quickly, he pressed his lips together in what looked like an angry slash, as his brows descended to meet nearly in a V between his eyes.

"Sit down and eat. I'm sorry if I made you uncomfortable," he said while morphing back to a man in control. He tugged at his shirt sleeve as if straightening his clothes would also recalibrate his demeanor.

The tone of his voice was the same as before—the one that rendered me helpless—almost. I took a measured step backward, then again, and once more until I bumped into my chair. Sinking down to the seat, I swiveled and faced my abandoned lunch. I couldn't be further from hungry now, so I studied the bread crust's contrast in color to the spongy white part and said nothing.

The sound of the creaky door caught my attention, and when I swung my gaze that way, it was only to see the back of my teacher as he bailed out like an ejecting fighter pilot.

I sat there alone for the longest ten minutes of my life, then finally fished my phone from my bag. I had to talk to someone just to get my mind to stop conjuring scenarios that ended in a multitude of ways other than what actually just happened. I fired off a text to my twin, making small talk to fill the stifling silence of the room.

Are you around?

About to go into my makeup chem final.
WUP?

While I sent text messages with proper punctuation and spelling, Shepperd had the slang and abbreviations of our generation mastered. Half the time when we communicated that way, I caught just a portion of what she said until I met up with her again and asked her what various letter combinations meant. Of course, that just annoyed her. Sometimes she would be gracious and explain the shorthand to me, and other times, she'd huff and roll her eyes and mutter some version of never mind.

Not much. I'm on a short lunch break and
wanted to be sure you made it to class.

Yes, Mom.

After failing to gauge her mood, I decided to wait until later to tell her what had happened. That sort of conversation seemed better for directly speaking to her than tapping out on my screen.

Well, good luck. I know you'll do great!

THX Mayday

And I was right back to where I started. Sitting alone in that deafeningly quiet room, staring at a sandwich I didn't want to eat. My phone alerted me of another incoming text after a few minutes, and my twin's face filled the screen.

You OK?

Yes, I'm fine. Go to class so you're not late.
I'll see you at home.

A genuine smile spread across my face from that two-word combination. There were a lot of things about my sister that people didn't know or understand. She had built a wall around herself over the past year—maybe a bit longer—and didn't let anyone get close. Except for me. She and I truly shared something special, and the fact that she noticed, just from the few lines I messaged, that something was bothering me made my heart swell.

I picked up my abandoned lunch and took a huge bite. I still wasn't hungry necessarily, but I never knew when Chaplin would give me a break, so I figured I'd eat while I had the opportunity. I finished the thing in a few more bites and was across the room throwing away my trash when the door opened.

"Andrew?" A woman poked her head in and called for my teacher. When she didn't get a reply, she came into the room farther and froze when she saw me.

"Hello," I said with a smile. "He's not here right now," I told her as though it were my place to speak on his whereabouts.

"I see," she said while doing one of those head-to-toe assessments. "And you are?"

I had no idea who the lady was, but I didn't appreciate her tone or the rude way she just sized me up. I must have hesitated long enough for her to rethink her behavior—or at least I hoped that was what prompted her next comment.

"I'm Rebecca Donnio. I'm a colleague of Professor Chaplin's," she explained nervously. "My office is next door, and I just popped in to see if he wanted to grab lunch."

"I'm not sure where he is. I think he may have gone to pick up some food. He didn't say before he left."

She shifted back to the ruder version of herself and said, "I'm sorry, dear, who are you?"

Pardon me? Dear? I despised when people used terms of endearment to be condescending. It was such a transparent tactic. Immature too.

My decent upbringing overrode my desire to tell this woman where she could stuff her territory marking.

Instead, I offered her my hand. "Hi. I'm Maye."

She shook my hand with the least bit of interest she could

feign. "Maye," she repeated and walked right past me and went to his desk and opened drawer after drawer until finding something to write on. I had no idea if they were good friends, or maybe more. Did they share a level of comfort that would excuse her invasion of his personal space?

She certainly thought so. I stood back and decided not to get involved. If he didn't want visitors in his office while he was gone, he should've made that known.

The woman watched while I took my seat. "I don't think I've seen you around campus before," she added while surreptitiously looking at the few things on his desk. Wow, this woman had some big balls to be snooping while I watched.

"Oh," was all I said but gave her a smile. Unfortunately, she was too preoccupied with her investigating to look at me. When I said nothing more, she finally met my stare.

"Are you looking for something in particular?" I asked. "I can let Dr. Chaplin know what you need when he returns," I said while holding her direct attention.

"No. Just leaving Andrew a little note here. I'm sure he'll see it right away." She strode to the door without giving me another glance.

I was too shocked at what I'd just witnessed to utter a goodbye.

I got back to work, assuming my instructor would return any moment. I'd rather be busy when he walked in than dawdling.

But I was wrong. It was just over an hour later when the man quietly entered the small office. I was fighting the need for a nap in the worst way, and he caught me mid-yawn when he came through the door.

"Pardon me," I said with a cautious smile. I waited until

he was settled behind his side of the desk to mention his visitor. "A woman came by looking for you. I believe she said she was one of your coworkers? She left a note for you on your desk." Rather than study him while delivering the message, I continued typing data into the spreadsheet I'd created.

He didn't respond to my information, and when I finally looked across the desk, he was staring at the folded note as though it were a poisonous snake. With one flat palm, he covered the paper, crumpled it into a ball, and dunked it right into the trash can beside our desk. Never opened it—just tossed it unread.

Well, I guess that's what he thinks of Ms. Donnio.

And why did I get so much pleasure out of that gesture? I told myself because of how rude she had been, but a nagging little voice inside my head called bullshit. I knew I'd been hoping he wasn't involved with that woman from the moment she'd poked her face in here. But I also knew I had no right to feel possessive of the guy who apparently couldn't stand to be in the same room with me for more than three hours.

After all, that was the second time he'd bolted from the office when the mood between us shifted. Maybe he was dealing with the same feelings I was and was uncomfortable about it. Even though there were no actual rules about staff dating students, it was frowned upon. Shep and I had actually researched the topic in the school's charter our freshman year. She had a hopeless crush on one of our professors that first year and came up with some insane plan to ask the guy out. It never worked out, though, because he disappeared over Christmas break, and a different teacher took over his classes when we returned for the second semester.

Professor Chaplin struck me as a rule-following kind of

guy, and the last thing I wanted was to cause problems for him.

So did I address the situation or just leave it? What if I were wrong? It would be so embarrassing to admit catching heavy lust for the man while he saw me as nothing more than a silly, inexperienced student.

Yeah, I'd just keep my nose in the books going forward and ignore whatever crazy ideas my libido was trying to lure me into. I was here to learn from the man and nothing more.

"I wanted to show you what I've been working on," I said while putting data into the last cell of the table. "Do you have a minute?" When I looked up to see why he hadn't answered, he was staring at me as though in a trance.

"Dr. Chaplin?"

He gave his head a little shake and refocused. "Sorry," he muttered.

"What are you apologizing for?"

"For staring at you. Again. For leaving so abruptly earlier. For leaving you here alone to deal with my nosy office neighbor," he rapidly listed and then paused like he wanted to add a fourth transgression.

"Oh, she's harmless, I'm sure." I chose to comment on the one thing that didn't have neon warning lights flashing around it.

He grunted a sort of laugh, but it was forced and manufactured and clearly not the topic weighing heaviest on his mind. "I hope you're right. I'm not sure how much clearer I can be to the woman that I'm not interested. I've told her at least three times this week."

"Maybe she needs a more obvious clue?" I offered before thinking. When he tilted his head marginally, I wanted to kick myself for opening my mouth at all.

"What do you mean?"

Boy, I really stuck my foot in my mouth now. Oh well, might as well go for broke. I shrugged first as though I were thinking of a solution on the fly. Truth be told, I'd been daydreaming about this most of my lunch break.

"I don't know. Maybe if she saw proof with her own eyes? Saw you in an intimate position with someone else?"

Chaplin's eyes widened to the size of nickels, and I laughed out loud. "Or not. I was just throwing out ideas."

"In theory, it's a decent idea. Seeing is believing, right? But the building is deserted this time of year. So unless you're volunteering for the lead actress role here, I'm out of luck."

I couldn't hide my grin. Or the flush recoloring my cheeks. Could I be bold enough to do it? "I could think of worse roles to play," I said sheepishly.

"Well, we'll see what happens. The university really discourages professors dating their students. She seems like the type of woman who could be really vindictive if rubbed the wrong way."

"She doesn't know I'm your intern. She was too busy snooping through your desk to be interested in anything about me. She didn't ask, and I didn't tell her. In fact, she said she'd never seen me around campus before."

"What did you just say?" he asked just as I finished speaking.

Confused, I repeated, "That she never saw me—"

But he interrupted with, "No, the part about my desk. Did you say she was looking through my desk?"

"Yes, sort of. She was looking for something to write the note on. But she was definitely noticing things while writing it, too." I sounded like a schoolgirl tattling on the playground.

"You've got to be kidding..."

I just shook my head. Suddenly I didn't want to be involved in this conversation anymore. He looked like he could spit nails. And in fairness, it was completely rude of her to do what she had.

The rest of the afternoon was more productive than just getting angry about Ms. Donnio. By the time I was walking out to the parking lot, I was exhausted. The last person I wanted to deal with was waiting on the sidewalk just outside the building.

If he hadn't seen me the moment I came outside, I would've turned back and hid inside until he gave up.

"There's the most beautiful girl on campus," Joel, my ex, said. His boyish smile used to be endearing. Now it gave me the creeps.

"Joel. What are you doing here? I thought you weren't taking any classes over the summer," I said, choosing not to even address his compliment. He was so over the top, it was hard to take seriously.

"I thought you might need a ride," he offered and approached for a hug.

I put my arm out to fend off the physical contact. "Shepperd is supposed to pick me up. Thanks, though." I couldn't force another smile today. Too many had already been manufactured for other people's comfort.

"Then can we talk until she gets here? I've really been thinking about us since the other day..." he began, but I stopped him mid-thought.

"Joel, listen. You really should move on, you know? Get back out into the dating pool and find someone better suited for you." There. That was gentle and kind, but at the same time, it was the bottom of the well for me. I didn't have one more nicety in my body for the guy. But he physically recoiled as though I'd stabbed him.

The guy grabbed me by the shoulders and gave me a solid shake. "No, Maye, I just want you."

I tried to throw his uninvited hands off, but he was gripping tight enough to bruise.

He continued with his desperate appeal. "And I've been thinking a lot about the things you said, and you're right. I can do better." Over his shoulder, I saw Professor Chaplin exit the building and zero right in on Joel and me.

"Oh, shit," I muttered, and it was enough to make him turn to see what I was reacting to. While he was distracted, I got out of his grip and took a step back, rubbing where I would surely have marks by bedtime.

My teacher rerouted his path to intercept us, and I held my breath while trying to predict what was about to happen.

I hated confrontation. Of any kind. I didn't particularly enjoy the scene between that woman and me in Chaplin's office today, and the potential of this personality collision was way worse. Anxiety churned my gut inside out.

"Is this boy bothering you, Ms. Farsey?" he asked sternly.

Instantly, Joel puffed out his chest and swung his whole body to face Chaplin.

Stupid boy. Don't do it.

But of course he did. "No, I'm not bothering her. She's my girlfriend, and we're talking," he said, looking like he held back a few choice words he wanted to add to the end.

I had to interject. "I'm not your girlfriend, Joel. We broke up. And I don't want to work on things, or whatever brought you here today. Please don't do this again." I felt proud of myself for not cowering to defuse the scene.

But what the hell was Chaplin playing at?

I would have never predicted him getting involved in my personal business. Though common decency would've directed any person with a shred of humanity in their soul to help when something didn't seem right.

Chaplin stared Joel down, but the guy was not backing off. I began to tell my ex to just leave, but my professor stepped between us. Physically wedged his body between Joel and me.

Fuck me sideways, the man never looked sexier than he did when he was coming to my rescue. Spurred into motion from the adrenaline spiking my system, I spun on my heel and power-walked away from the men. If they were about to go to blows, I didn't want to witness it.

I'd gotten halfway across the greenbelt when I heard Chaplin calling my name. "Maye! Stop!"

Over my shoulder, I saw him in quick pursuit. He had covered half the distance I'd gained with my head start and was closing the rest of the gap.

"Just wait a minute," he shouted. I wanted to obey his command and continue fleeing at the same time.

Unfortunately, because I wasn't watching where I was going, I tripped over a protruding root of one of the ancient oak trees and went down like a sack of potatoes.

Luckily, I braced for myself impact, or I would've been Googling emergency dental offices. But when I got my wits back about me and looked at my throbbing palms, both were skinned and bleeding.

"For Christ's sake," I clearly heard him say as he squatted down to survey the damage. "Are you okay?" Before I could respond, he grabbed both wrists and turned my hands so he could inspect for himself.

Pain that felt way too intense for just the scrapes I suffered bolted through my entire right arm, and I cried out. Professor Chaplin loosened his grip but didn't release me completely as he studied my face with great concern.

"Where does it hurt?" he demanded. I tried to pull away again, but he wouldn't relent. "Answer me, damn it, Maye."

"My arm," I whimpered. "My whole arm hurts. Really bad." Tears filled my eyes, and I couldn't be more embarrassed. Through the pain, I croaked, "It hurts all the way up to my shoulder. I must have landed harder than I thought."

His face shifted from the panic that was there just moments before to genuine concern. "Let me help you up. We should probably have it looked at."

Out of habit, I disagreed. We were taught from early childhood to tough it out. Not every little scratch or scrape was cause for a scene. With a house full of females, my father made sure we weren't frail little damsels in distress.

"No, that's not necessary. I'm sure it's fine," I insisted. But oh my God, it hurt so badly I had to choke back the tears that were blurring my vision. "I'm sure it's fine," I repeated, trying to convince myself as much as him.

"Here, take my arm with the good one, and we'll get you on your feet." He thrust his forearm toward me to assist, but I was nothing if not stubborn. I put the slightest weight on both wrists to balance while I stood up, and again, the right arm felt like a bolt of lightning struck me to the bone.

"Fuck!" I shouted and toppled to the side. Andrew was right there, thankfully, and he steadied me until I had my body under control. Tears streaked my cheeks in the early evening heat, and the whole world seemed to be spinning in the wrong direction. My head felt gauzy and thick, and darkness closed in from the edges.

I was going to pass out if I didn't get my head lower than my heart as soon as possible.

"Whoa there, baby. Let's sit down right here on this bench," he said in a new tone I'd never heard from the man. Could've also been my mind playing tricks on me without the requisite amount of blood supply. "You're white as a sheet," he continued to insist while guiding me down to the wrought-iron park bench.

Did he really just call me *baby?*

Basic first aid knowledge kicked in, and I widened my knees to make room for my head. I bent forward and hung there for a solid minute, willing the world to stop the tilt-a-whirl impression it was pulling. While in that position, my teacher gently stroked his hand down my spine. Over and over, and it was so kind and comforting.

Finally, I slowly sat upright and looked directly at the man beside me. He was worried and maybe a little pissed, if I read his expression correctly. Couldn't say I blamed him, either.

Joel, the little dickhead, was nowhere to be seen. It was obvious I was looking around the grounds, and Andrew grew noticeably impatient.

"He drove off. The little shit drove away when you took off." And I thought I heard him say, "I can't believe you dated that idiot," under his breath.

For some reason, that pissed me off. With a good amount of attitude, I thrust my hand to my hip to confront him, but the pain was unbearable.

I was really hurt. There was no denying it. If Shepperd had pulled up while we were here in the common, she would've driven off when I wasn't there waiting in front of the office building. She was as impatient as she was irritable, and she never waited around for anyone.

"Did you see anyone else drive up?" I asked my attentive instructor. "My twin?" I added out of habit and to further explain what I was asking. "She was supposed to pick me up after our day was finished."

Slowly, we started walking back toward the parking lot. I cradled my throbbing arm against my chest to immobilize the injury and measured every step before taking it. If I fell again, it would be ten times worse.

At first, he just shook his head. After we navigated around another root, he said, "No, there haven't been any cars. In the lot or on the street since I first came out of the building."

We slowly covered more ground, and he asked, "You have a twin?" It truly sounded like he was hearing the information for the first time.

When you were a twin, it seemed like everyone knew. Even before they knew your name or any other detail about you, they knew you were half of a whole.

If I weren't already in miserable pain, I'd kick myself for mentioning it. I'd be shocked, though, if this man launched into the list of stupid questions we always got when people first made our acquaintance. He was so much better than that.

When he began speaking, I realized I'd given him too much credit.

"I didn't realize," he started, and I rolled my eyes, not caring if he saw the gesture or not. But he was undeterred. Of course, he was. However, he narrowed his gaze as he continued, "I didn't realize you had siblings. And why are you rolling your eyes?"

While I was relieved he didn't disappoint me and fall into

the same routine everyone else did, making small talk with Andrew was unusual.

"Yes. I have four sisters," I said and decided to leave it at that.

"You need medical attention. I'll take you. That's my car over there," he announced as though he had a say in what I did next.

I stopped walking, feeling steadier now that we were on the blacktop of the parking lot, and looked at him. "That's not necessary. It's fine," I said for the third time, knowing he didn't believe it any more than I did.

"It's really swelling. I think you broke something. You can't drive, and I won't allow you to get into a car with some random rideshare person while you're defenseless. Please don't continue arguing."

"I'm not defenseless, and it's very presumptuous of you to think you can decide what I need and what I don't." The agonizing pain in my arm was making me surly, and I didn't care. This day had officially gone to shit, and I didn't have it in me to fake being sweet for one more minute.

As though I never spoke, he guided me to the passenger side of his car and blocked me from going anywhere other than into the car.

"Get in, Maye. I'll help you with the seat belt."

"That won't be necessary," I said, and a deep, promising growl came from his chest.

And hit me bull's-eye between the legs.

What the hell? Can't say that ever happened before...over a tone of voice... Or was it the command behind it?

But I also never tolerated a man speaking to me the way he had. I knew my two older sisters liked a bossy kind of guy, and I always thought I didn't. But I was also never involved with someone who was man enough to try.

CHAPTER SEVEN

ANDREW

My patience wore away like the banks along a rushing stream with every insistence she was fine. She wasn't fine. She was hurt, and it was my fault. If I'd kept my damn possessiveness in check with that dipshit kid, she wouldn't have run off. Plus, because she was upset when she bolted, she was careless with her route.

Through gritted teeth, I issued, "Damn it, Maye. Get in the car, or I'll pick you up and put you there myself. I already feel completely responsible for your injury. I won't let you do further harm by not having it looked at." My voice was calm and direct and about two octaves deeper than normal.

Her blue eyes, glassy from the tears she kept trying to choke back, were fixed on my mouth, and fuck if it wasn't spiking my arousal. I was such a bastard.

I shook my head with self-aimed disgust, and the motion crushed her focus on my mouth.

"What?" she croaked, and the pitiful sound of her inquiry pinned me to the parking lot blacktop.

"I'm just..." I began and quickly stopped myself. I couldn't tell her all the things running through my mind. How I wanted to knock that boy's head off his shoulders for manhandling her. How I wanted to take her back to my place and care for her through the night. How I couldn't stop wondering about what it would feel like to kiss her.

"It's just that..." I began again but still had nothing appropriate to say. Instead, I motioned once more with a sweep of my arm for her to get into the car. Thank God, she finally complied. I perched on the door frame with half my ass and reached across her to grab the safety belt.

It was then I was struck square in the chest by that damn morning glory scent of hers. Maye watched me carefully as I battled the effects of her nearness and finally pulled the belt from her shoulder to the opposite hip.

"Lift up a bit please," I said, trying desperately to ignore how close we were. I could kiss her right now. I was inches from that pouty, defiant, stubborn, independent mouth, and I wanted to kiss her more than take my next breath. When I was foolish enough to meet her curious stare again, our noses were nearly touching. I froze there for longer than I should have, involved in a full-scale war with my better judgment.

Finally, I whispered, "I'm sorry."

"For what?" Her voice was low and raspy, and I let my lids fall closed and savored the resonant sound. But just for a beat or two, because I couldn't pass up the chance to be so close to her and not take in every detail I could catalog.

She had freckles on her nose and the very tops of her cheeks. Not many, and it looked like she tried to cover them with some sort of makeup trick. Now that she had been crying, vertical streaks marked each side, and I could see them clearly.

"For what?" she repeated, and this time I was the one to physically shake my head to snap out of the fog our proximity created.

"Your arm. That...that...guy." I thumbed over my shoulder

as though he were still standing there in the empty parking lot. The few cars that were here when I'd first come out were gone now. The first lights around campus began to flicker on with the emerging nightfall.

She smiled cautiously, and my heart lurched up into my throat and stuck there. She was arrestingly beautiful in the evening light.

"It wasn't your fault. I tripped," she said softly. "I've always been the clumsy one." She laughed lightly, but it was forced. I didn't like her saying anything negative about herself and immediately thought to disagree.

But I had to move away from her. If I stayed there a moment longer, I would lose control. The majority of my fantasies about this young woman always began with her pouty lips. Now that she'd been crying, they were even fuller and were an inviting, darker rose hue. All I could think of was biting her there, and I was so close to doing it, I jolted from the door frame.

My erratic movement must have startled her, and by the time I was around to the driver's side and climbing in, she was struggling to unlatch the seat belt to get out. Calmly, I put my much larger hand atop hers to still her.

Gently, I asked, "What are you doing?"

"This really isn't necessary. I just need to call for a ride so I can get home and...and...I don't know," she stammered, then shrugged and immediately winced from the pain the gesture caused. "Ice it or something. Take something for the pain and swelling..." She trailed off while staring at my hand covering hers.

Neither one of us pulled away, and I grew bold. I swept her fingers into mine and turned to face her in my seat. "Listen to me. I won't take no for an answer. You can either let me take you to the urgent care about two miles from here, or you can come back to my house, and I will tend to it myself. Of course, I can't x-ray it, and I really think that's what you need, but those are your choices. I won't allow you to leave my company without knowing this has been properly cared for."

Holy. Fuck. What the hell did I just offer? Better than that, would she take me up on it? The words came out of my mouth without any input from my brain. Clearly. I was walking a tightrope here with no net below. One wrong—or right—word from the student in my passenger seat, and everything would become as unpredictable as a three-ring big top. Now that I issued the ultimatum, though, there was no way in hell I'd take it back.

"Your place?" she murmured. I couldn't tell if she was mulling over the option when the words slipped past her lips, or if that was her actual answer. The man in me decided to not wait around to find out. I snapped my seat belt into place, started the engine, and pulled out of the parking lot before she could think better of what she'd just agreed to.

Thankfully, I didn't live too far from campus, and traffic was almost nonexistent because we were going in the opposite direction of most commuters. At first, the silence in the car was suffocating. Every attempt I made at speaking got lodged behind that ball of lust still stuck in my throat. A few times she looked like she was about to say something too but then clamped her lips together and sank deeper into the bucket seat.

At the exact same moment, we both gave it one more try.

"Are you hungry?" I asked.

"Is this a good idea?" she wondered at the precise time.

"No," I said just as she offered the same reply. Obviously,

we were answering different questions, but the responses fit both. Our grins were matching then too, and I gave her hand a little reassuring pat.

I wouldn't do anything she was uncomfortable with. Of course I wouldn't. But she didn't know that. She was taking an incredible risk going to a stranger's house. If we were truly in a relationship, I'd spank her ass for being so reckless.

And that was a thought I didn't have the luxury of letting bloom any further in my imagination. At least not while driving and trying to keep my wits about me. Just a few more blocks and we'd reach my residential neighborhood. I could behave myself until we could get a little more space between us.

Honestly, though, I didn't want to behave. I wanted to do unspeakable things to defile the stunning woman frozen in the seat beside me. My dick swelled to an uncomfortable state, and no amount of shifting relieved the pressure. It was possible her unease was fueling my fire, and she didn't even realize it. Something about her measured innocence spoke to the darkest places inside me. I wanted to teach her and cherish her at the same time.

We pulled into my quaint neighborhood with tree-lined, quiet streets and charming one-story, old California-style homes. When I purchased the house, it was that very same throwback vibe the entire three-block expanse of houses gave off that spoke to me. The architectural style was understated and comforting and reminded me of a simpler time. These homes were built long before the bigger-is-better real estate mentality took over. Each one was unique and interesting, and I never regretted the purchase. I figured if I ever outgrew the place, whether because I started a family or just needed more room to spread out, I'd keep this place as a rental. It was the perfect starter home or retirement place.

Maye studied the bungalow through the windshield and didn't give a hint as to what she thought of it. She still cradled her injured arm against her chest, reminding me instantly of why we were here. I needed to take care of her.

Out of the driver's seat without a word, I hustled to her side, opened the door, and leaned across her to unlatch the seat belt. I heard her inhale sharply and quickly pulled back, thinking I'd jostled her arm inadvertently.

"Oh, sorry. I'll go slower," I vowed, and she gave me a quick smile. "Let's get you inside."

"No, it's fine, honest. I can do it," she said when I offered help to get out, so I forced myself to step back and give her that independence. Her bag tumbled off her lap and onto the driveway, and I bent to pick it up for her before she even realized what happened.

"I'll carry this. You just keep that stable," I said and motioned to her arm with my chin. Closing her door behind her, I hit the lock icon on the key fob and escorted her to the front door.

"Sorry if the place is a bit unkempt. I left in a hurry this morning," I apologized while maneuvering the key into the lock. I swung the heavy door open and swept my arm out for her to lead us inside. I watched her quickly scan the entrance and front room before I locked the door behind us. I hoped we wouldn't be leaving for the rest of the night, so I locked the deadbolt too.

I led her through the living room and into the kitchen. There was a small island in the center with three stools along the longer side. "Do you want to sit here while I get an ice pack together?"

"I have a choice now?" she asked with a raised brow and pulled one of the stools back with her foot. I decided not to address the comment and busied myself with a Ziploc bag and the ice maker.

"I'll get you something for the pain too, but I think it would be better with a little something in your stomach. You barely ate lunch," I continued but stopped babbling when she tilted her head at my observation.

"What?"

"You watch how much I eat?" she asked with disbelief. "You weren't even in the room."

"Honestly, Ms. Farsey." Pausing there, I leaned toward her across the island with my chin propped on one bent arm. "I can't stop watching everything you do." My response was bolder and my tone much darker than she was expecting, because she immediately looked away. But I was done tiptoeing around my attraction to her. Now that we were in the privacy of my home, I wanted to drop the confines of our teacher-student association and get to know the woman before me.

"Does that make you uncomfortable? Saying that?" I asked while sliding the ice pack toward her. "That swelling really looks awful," I muttered.

"It looks worse than it feels," she said while opening and closing her fist. When I gave her a skeptical look, she added, "Honestly, it's just throbbing. It will probably be good as new by morning." She forced a beaming smile, and the whole display pissed me off.

Why did she feel like she had to hide behind the ruse of perfection all the time? I'd bet my paycheck the thing was badly sprained if not broken. At that point, I couldn't even tell if it was her wrist or arm that suffered the damage, since the entire arm had ballooned.

Then she surprised me by addressing the other question I asked. "No, you don't make me uncomfortable." She grinned. "Confused?" she asked and then immediately answered, "Definitely. But not uncomfortable."

"I confuse you?" I asked with a hint of incredulity.

"Well, at first, I really thought you didn't like me. At all. But then I see you watching me while I'm working, and yeah, that confuses me. I'm not sure what's going on here." Then she added in case I wasn't clear on the meaning of the last part, "Between us."

"I'd like to speak openly with you," I began while cautiously peeking at her reaction. "I'm going to fix you something to eat so you can take something for the pain. What sounds good?" Then I thought about it more. "Although I have limited options here. Bachelor living and all," I explained while opening the refrigerator. After scanning its contents, the best I could offer was a cup of yogurt or maybe a grilled cheese sandwich if the bread in the pantry was still usable. Maye swiveled on the stool to follow me around the kitchen while I came up with some options.

"Okay, looks like strawberry yogurt or grilled cheese. Either of those sound appealing?" I asked sheepishly. It was a tone I did my best to stay clear of on principle, but I was embarrassed to not be able to provide for her. "Not very impressive, I realize," I mumbled while waiting for her decision.

"What will you have? You need food as much as I do. I haven't seen you eat all day. Though, you did go missing around lunch, so maybe you ate then?"

Her comment stopped my pointless shuffling around the

kitchen, and I met her waiting gaze. I owed her an explanation for my irregular behavior. I just hoped she could handle the truth. I wouldn't survive the summer dancing around my attraction to her without knowing how she felt. But Christ, it was so risky. Just laying my feelings out in front of her and letting her decide our fate. Or mine, if nothing else.

"I'm sorry I took off without explaining where I was going. It was rude and, honestly, a little immature. I couldn't be confined in that small office with you for one more minute and be responsible for my actions."

She tilted her head, repositioned the ice pack, and asked, "Your actions? What does that mean?"

I came to stand right in front of her. I wanted her to hear the sincerity in what I was about to admit. "Maye, listen. Plain and simply put, I'm attracted to you. Really attracted to you." I repeated my confession as if saying it over and over was the only way to make peace with it. "When we're in that confined space, I start to go a little batty wanting to do things to you that I'm not sure you want too."

Her deep-blue eyes found mine, and I couldn't quite read her wide expression.

"Oh," was all she said, and panic rose from my stomach. Did I just fuck up by telling her that so bluntly?

"Just oh?" I said, hoping to encourage her to express herself more.

"Well, that's a pretty bold admission. I'm trying to take it all in for a second before I admit I've been feeling the same way," she replied, and the first part of her comment almost got overshadowed by the second.

Until I repeated it back in my head, and then said through my grin, "You do?" I couldn't stifle my smile. Or my dick, apparently, because that fucker heard her words loud and clear and was swelling with anticipation.

She quickly nodded but couldn't hold my gaze. She maneuvered the ice-filled bag again.

"Maye, look at me," I said with a voice so dark and lust-filled, it even took me by surprise. Those big, innocent, sapphire eyes found mine, and I tried to read what other emotions I saw there.

"What's wrong? You look like there's more you want to say," I prompted.

"Well, it's wrong to feel that way, isn't it? I don't want to get you in trouble with the university. And I can't afford to lose this opportunity. I can handle myself, though, I swear. I just don't want you to say we have to stop the internship."

"The school doesn't have a policy against teachers and students dating. It's not something they like, per se, but it's not an infraction that would end my employment there. I don't want to put you in an uncomfortable situation, though, so I thought being honest would be the best approach here."

"I appreciate that," she said with a bolder smile then. "I really do. I definitely thought I was picking up some energy between us, and in the same spirit of honesty, I find it very exciting. But it's also become very distracting, and we're not even through week one."

"You're very mature for your age. Very articulate," I said and took a couple of steps closer to her. It wasn't a decision I made. My body just took over and did what it wanted. I needed to touch her.

Standing directly in front of her, I offered a hand to her uninjured one and tugged her to her feet. "One last thing, then I feed you. No arguments." She focused on my mouth while I spoke in that way a woman did when she was hoping you'd kiss her. My cock actually lurched in my slacks.

"What is it?" she began, but I cut her off with my kiss. I didn't want to spook her, but there was no way I could withstand another minute without feeling those full lips against mine.

Heaven. She was fucking heaven in so many ways. The way her lithe body melted into mine, the way her plush mouth yielded to mine, the little whimpers coming from low in her throat. Our kiss grew in depth and urgency until I finally broke away or I'd lay her across my kitchen island and mount her.

Well...that thought had promise.

When we separated, her delicate fingers reached up and touched her mouth, as if she couldn't believe what just happened.

"The look on your face says I should apologize," I said, but a grin that I couldn't hold back revealed I wouldn't mean it. "But I'm not sorry. Not in the least."

"No," she said so quietly it was more like air moving than sound. "Don't be sorry. I'm glad you did that." The same grin infected her then too. "I hope it happens again, actually."

I took a measured step back, or I'd be on her before she could object. "No," I told myself as much as her. "First, you need to eat so you can take something for that arm. After that?" I let the pause between thoughts inflate a bit. "All bets are off."

I probably secured my place in hell with that declaration, but I'd make this girl mine. That little shit that had been hanging around her would become a distant memory, and she would wonder what she ever saw in that silly boy in the first place.

CHAPTER EIGHT

MAYE

Watching Andrew move around his tidy kitchen was fascinating. I was seeing a whole new side of the man that I would have never thought existed. He was still very measured in everything he did. Even the kiss he planted on me was as careful as it was reckless. And my God, was it reckless.

There was a very loud, annoying voice in my head screaming at me to put the brakes on here. Stop this crazy behavior before it became something we couldn't step around. I had to spend the entire summer with this man, and watching him flip a grilled cheese sandwich in a bright-blue frying pan was the only thing I could bother myself with now. The voice could seriously fuck off, as far as I was concerned. Even if it was the voice of reason or better judgment, I was so tired of always doing the right thing. The safe thing.

I wanted to be reckless for once. If I needed further proof of how tired I was of safe and smart, all I had to do was reflect on the relationship I just ended. The main reason I got out of that pairing was because I was bored to tears with the guy. And what the hell was he thinking today, putting his hands on me the way he had? Subconsciously I pressed my fingertips into the spot where I suspected a bruise had formed, and sure enough, the skin was tender there. If my father ever found out that dumbass laid hands on me that way, he'd skin him alive.

My cellphone played Shepperd's ringtone from deep inside my handbag. I had a little trouble fishing it out with just one hand, so by the time I tried to accept her call, it had gone to voicemail. I'd be shocked if she actually left a message, but now that I was staring at the thing, I saw that she had tried calling several times before.

"Oh shit," I muttered, and Andrew turned from the stove.

"What's wrong?"

"My sister has been trying to call, and I missed her three times. Well, make that four with the one I just heard. Do you mind if I call her? She's probably worried because I wasn't at school when she came to pick me up."

"Of course not. Do you need help?" he asked gently, and I really thought to pinch myself. He was such a different man than the teacher I knew in class. I really liked this version of my professor. A grin refused to budge as I dialed my twin.

"Oh, my fucking God, Maye! Are you trying to give me a heart attack?"

"Hello to you, too," I greeted my frantic sister.

"Maye," she nearly shouted for the second time, and guilt flooded my entire being.

"Shep, calm down. What's going on? You okay?"

"Yes, I'm okay. Where the hell are you? I waited at school for like twenty minutes. Are you still inside? I'll head back."

Shit. I hadn't really thought this through. What was I going to tell her? I couldn't tell her I was at Professor Chaplin's house. Although, she'd be the one person in my life to give this whole craziness two thumbs up.

"No, I left. Joel showed up—"

"Oh no, Maye. Don't tell me you're back with that loser."

"You didn't let me finish," I chided. "He showed up while I was waiting for you, and when I told him to go away? No kidding, Shep...he got physical with me." I whispered that last part because I could barely admit it happened. And that in itself made me so angry. Why did I feel guilty when he was the one who was so out of line? It didn't make sense, and rationally, I knew that. Yet here I was, feeling embarrassed as though it was my fault.

"You can't be serious right now," she gasped. "What did you do? Knee him in the dick, I hope."

"No, he ran off when Professor Chaplin came out of the building and got in his face."

I could picture her salacious expression when she asked, "Ooooh, did they actually brawl?"

"No," I said immediately, and I could almost hear her excitement deflate. "Joel took off."

The line was quiet for a moment while she put all the pieces together. "Okay, so where the fuck are you?"

I stood up and walked into the front room. I wanted a little privacy while I explained to my sister what was going on. "Well, it's kind of a long story. I fell and really hurt my arm, so he brought me back to his house."

"He who? Chaplin? For real?" Her questions came faster than I could answer and louder than I was expecting. Not sure if it was the general quiet of this house or if Shepperd was shouting.

"Shut. The. Front. Door," she continued, emphasizing each word with her disbelief.

"Please don't tell Mom and Dad, okay?" I waited for her to agree. "Shep? Okay?"

"Why would I tell them? I don't even speak to them unless

I have to." If I hadn't been standing in my teacher's living room, I'd dive deeper into that remark. Every relationship she currently had was in disrepair because of her surly attitude. Except ours. That worried me and comforted me at the same time.

"Thank you," was all I came up with at first. "I'm not really sure when I'll be home. Cover for me?" I asked sheepishly. I wasn't used to being dishonest, and it didn't feel good inside. I wasn't doing anything wrong necessarily. So why was guilt doing a magnificent two-step all over my conscience?

"Duh. You know I got your back." Then she began calculating. I could hear it in the way her voice shifted when she finished with, "Only if you give me every single detail when I see you."

I laughed with relief. "You got it. Thanks, sister."

"Have fun. Don't do anything I wouldn't do," she advised.

"And what does that leave?" I teased back. This was an ongoing bit we had between us. Or used to have. My sister rarely joked anymore.

"Nothing!" She cackled, and it was the most animated I had heard her in a long time.

I hung up and went back to the kitchen with a big smile still on my face. Andrew had set a place mat and napkin at the spot I'd been sitting, and also the spot right beside it. He was walking around the island from the stove as I came back into the room, a plate in each hand.

"Smells good." I smiled and took my seat gingerly. My whole body was starting to ache, and I was anxious to take something for the pain.

"Everything okay?" he asked and motioned to my phone with his chin.

"Yes, thank you. My sister was supposed to pick me up after school today. She freaked out a bit when I wasn't there, but she's good now."

"Please start eating. I'll get you something for the pain. You're moving very carefully, and I'm guessing it's getting worse?"

Instead of admitting he was right, I just dipped my chin and reached for the sandwich with my left hand. Everyday things were going to be a real hassle with my dominant arm immobilized.

I had only taken a couple of bites by the time he returned. His gaze switched back and forth between my plate and me before he asked, "Is it not good? I'm not much of a cook, but it's pretty hard to screw up grilled cheese."

If possible, he looked even more handsome while admitting a possible shortcoming. While I doubted the man couldn't master anything he attempted, I said nothing. Just picked up the sandwich and took another bite. The truth was that my nerves and the pain were causing a riot in my stomach. I didn't want to eat in the first place, but he was being so insistent.

"Take these." He handed me two pills, and I threw them in my mouth without even looking at them.

"Thank you, Andrew. For everything. You really didn't have to go through all the—"

"I absolutely did. We've been over this already. I feel responsible for you falling and wouldn't have felt right driving off while you stood there injured." He sat on his stool and turned to face me. He swiveled my seat to face him and bracketed my knees with his. "I'll take you home when you're finished if you'd like." He studied me before admitting, "But, baby, I'd really like you to stay."

This directness was so refreshing. I wasn't sure if it was his certainty, or experience, or what gave him the confidence to be so blunt, but it was so different from guys my own age.

And he called me baby *again.*

I had never been a big fan of pet names. In my family, the nicknames were abundant, but I'd never had one from a partner. Something about the way he said the simple term flooded me with warmth and arousal at the same time. He stared at me like he expected a reply, so I swallowed and smiled softly.

"Does that smile mean you'll stay?" he asked with the hope of a little boy.

My voice was husky when I managed to say, "Yes, I would like to stay if it's not too much of a burden. I can sleep on the couch, no problem."

He tilted his head to one side, reminding me so much of Hannah's husband, Elijah. Except Andrew's hair was trimmed close, so there was no messy tumble of hair when he did it.

Just sharp, angular facial features and a gaze so intense, I felt like I'd combust in the middle of his kitchen. Maybe I wasn't woman enough to handle this guy. Feeling inadequate was a serious flaw of mine. Situations like this were fuel to my insecure fire.

When my twin and I were infants, Hannah, our oldest sister, was the victim of a kidnapping attempt in our neighborhood Target. After that, our parents went off the deep end protecting us. What it really turned into was sheltering us, so natural confidence just wasn't something I had. I understood why they became so neurotic about our safety, but there were a lot of times I suffered socially because of it.

I didn't really start dating until our senior year of high

school. And really, I only did at that point because all the social norms were passing me by. Homecoming, prom, graduation parties, and the like usually required a date or interaction with boys. It didn't help, once again, that I was the invisible twin. Shepperd had a personality big enough for both of us, and oftentimes I faded into the background.

All that introspection removed me from conversation with the alluring man right in front of me. A slow smile crept across my lips when I took in the whole situation. How the hell was I sitting in my professor's kitchen, intermittently picturing him without his clothes?

"Where did you drift off to just then?" he asked, voice still deep and intense.

"Oh." I laughed lightly. "So many places. My head is a busy, busy place, you see."

"I imagine it is. I think you have so much potential, Maye. I hope this doesn't make you want to end our summer arrangement."

Why would he think that? Maybe he really saw me as a whimsical teen even though I was about to turn twenty-three. Maybe he thought I wouldn't be able to separate a personal relationship from the one we had to uphold at school.

"How old are you?" I asked before I could lose the nerve. He physically recoiled at the question, though, and I instantly wished I could take it back.

"Does our age gap bother you?" he asked instead of answering my question.

"No, not at all. I've always gotten along better with people older than me." I shrugged while trying to pinpoint why that might be. "I just relate better. Seem to have more in common."

"I believe that," he said after finishing the last bite of his sandwich.

Wow! He powered through that thing while I barely finished half of mine.

"You didn't answer my question, though." I looked at him skeptically. "Did you think I wouldn't notice?"

"Wouldn't notice the age difference?" he asked, and I thought it was his attempt at humor because there was a twinkle in his eye that wasn't usually there. Normally, his eyes were dark and soulful, but now they were bright and lively.

"Cute." I leaned toward him, my body subconsciously seeking more of what he treated it to before. "I meant the way you evaded my question."

"No, baby, I knew it wouldn't sneak past you." He swept my good hand into his and placed it on his chest.

I sneaked a quick exploration of the toned muscle beneath my palm, and my blood pressure spiked again. Swaying toward him, I willed him to plant another kiss on me. I wanted it more than anything.

"Eat," he insisted instead and casually stood and made his way back to the stove to clean up. I had to press my lips together to ensure the whimper he caused when withdrawing didn't slip out. It could've been in response to the obvious bulge in his pants, too.

"You're a bit of a tease, Professor," I accused in my best formal speech.

"The reality is, I don't trust myself when we are so close. I want to do unspeakable things to you, Maye Farsey, and I'm doing my very best not to frighten you." He said it all so plainly, like we were discussing the bread on the plate in front of me.

"I'm not inexperienced, Andrew. You're not going to scare me." I chuckled then because really, men were men, no matter their age. Apparently he held his sexual prowess in high regard, as a lot of guys seemed to do.

"Are you amused?" he asked in an even darker tone.

"A little, yes," I said and sucked in a fuller breath when I met his intense stare.

Quickly I added, "But not by you specifically. More of a private conversation going on in here." I tapped my temple while he carefully listened.

A girl could really get used to this level of attention. Was this another difference between men his age and the boys mine? The guys I had dated in the past were more interested in themselves than anything else. You would think after spending that much time only considering themselves, they'd have a better understanding of who they truly were. What they wanted. Maybe the by-product of all that self-focus when younger was the sure, sexy, self-aware man before me.

There were so many things to consider from just the few hours I'd spent in his presence. I was thrilled intellectually and, my God, so damn aroused physically. After a few more bites of the sandwich, I pushed it away a few inches.

"Thank you so much for feeding me. It was delicious." I smiled until I met his steady gaze and the stern appearance of the rest of his features. "What's wrong?" I asked, and it came out sounding like a pitiful croak.

"Finish what's on your plate, please. It was one sandwich. Not even a full meal."

His whole tone rubbed me the wrong way. I looked at him for a few seconds before having to look away. His stare was so intense, he reduced me to a nervous, ungrateful child, and I didn't appreciate any of it.

"Listen," I began and barely had the courage to say more.

I swallowed the lump that had formed in my throat and forced the rest of my thought out in words. "I have a mother and a father. I'm not in the market for another parent-figure in my life. I'm twenty-two years old and am fully aware of when I'm full. I don't want you to think I'm ungrateful for the food you gave me. I just can't eat more than that right now." After giving it a bit more thought, I finished my little speech with, "Especially after the evening I've had. My stomach can't handle any more."

"Okay." He nodded but didn't look impressed with any of what I'd just said. In fact, his mood seemed to turn a bit sour.

"I can call my sister to come pick me up," I offered and began to dig for my phone. "Can you tell me the address?"

He rounded the island to stand in front of me quickly and gracefully, completely catching me off guard.

Andrew planted a hand on the stool by each side of my thighs and spun me away from the island. Leaning closer, he nearly growled, "Parenting you is the very last thing I had in mind, Maye."

I paused a few beats to let the meaning of his words sink in.

"I'd like you to stay but won't force you to. If I've made you uncomfortable, or unhappy, I apologize. Whether you believe me or not, my wanting you to eat is from my concern for your system and the pain reliever I gave you," he explained matter-of-factly. "That was stronger than your average over-the-counter stuff, and I don't want it to hit you too hard because you've barely eaten all day."

This was definitely going to take some work. Time and patience, too. Yes, he was older than me, but that didn't always mean he knew what was best for me. My parents raised me to be an independent woman, and I didn't need a babysitter to ensure I took care of myself.

I just had to figure out a way to get him to understand that.

CHAPTER NINE

ANDREW

Fine. Maybe that was a little much. She'd either get used to it or run in the opposite direction. One thing was for certain—I wasn't likely to change at this point in my life. My personality always fell into the domineering category. Even as a young boy, my mother said I was a leader, not a follower. Didn't mean I couldn't successfully be a part of a group. It just wasn't my naturally preferred place.

Now if I were the group's leader, then I was in my element. I did my best work and was most creative and thoughtful as the guy in charge.

Concentrating on the fresh-faced woman before me while she made herself clear on a few points wasn't difficult. I could be laser-focused when something mattered to me. And this girl mattered. She mattered in more ways than I fully identified with yet, but my gut knew she would become an important point of light on my horizon. I'd always trusted my intuition, so it was easy to give her all my attention and ensure we laid a solid foundation from the start.

The big-picture goal was that a true relationship could come of this insane physical attraction we shared, and along the way, we'd discover all the things we had in common and could celebrate.

Maybe I should feel embarrassed about how much thought I'd already given all this. But I'd had Maye in class for a full semester. Tons of time to observe her in different situations, listen to the way her mind worked when we had an open discussion in class, and learn what a truly kind and genuine human she was.

It might seem like I'd made plans based on our short time together in my office, but that wasn't the case at all. From the moment she'd taken her front-row, far-left seat in my class, she'd stolen my breath, focus, and, very recently, my careful control.

"Now it's my turn to ask you where you drifted off to?" she asked while standing. She picked up her plate, and I instantly took it from her grip.

She huffed. "I can clear my own dishes. You did the cooking. It's the least I can do."

"Please, just relax," I offered in easy rebuttal to her intentions. "As you yourself said, it's been a trying evening. I'll take care of this."

"My parents raised me better than that," she said while following me to the sink with our place mats and glasses.

"I'm sure they did, but I insist." I took the mats from her and stole a peck on those sinful lips. My action took her by surprise, and I grinned, watching her process what had just happened.

When a slow smile spread across her face, I turned toward the sink and piled the few dishes in. I'd worry about loading the dishwasher later.

"Would you like to watch a movie or something?" I asked, motioning toward my living room. My house wasn't very large, but the space was used wisely, and it always felt bigger to me than it was. With Maye here, I wondered what she saw as she looked around.

"Can we just sit and talk? I'd like to get to know you better. Especially outside that little office. Have you always wanted to teach?"

"Yes and no," I answered as we sat on the sofa. She sat farther away than I wanted, so I patted the cushion beside me. "Sit closer. I won't bite." I thought about that for a second, and my dick perked up. "Well, never mind that. I shouldn't make promises."

She scooted closer, and I angled my body toward her. With my arm slung across the back cushions, I gently touched her hair. I'd been longing to do that every time she'd worn it down, and it was as silky as I'd imagined it would be.

"You are so beautiful, Maye," I said before I lost the nerve.

"Thank you. You're so sweet," she said automatically. Clearly the response of a woman used to compliments. It was the robotic tone that pulled me out of the moment, and I dropped my hand.

She turned more to face me. "What's wrong?"

"Nothing. How's the arm?" I figured it wasn't worth accusing her of something I didn't quite understand and risk getting into a disagreement. She flip-flopped from easygoing to defensive pretty quickly, and I didn't like it. Walking on eggshells was a terrible existence, though, so I reminded myself to slow down a bit. It was possible my aggressive approach was partially to blame for her defensiveness.

"I think the pain reliever is starting to kick in. Thank you again for whatever that was. I must say, though, I'm feeling pretty sleepy all of a sudden." On cue, her body offered an exceptionally long yawn, and she giggled behind her hand.

"God, excuse me. It may just be this comfortable sofa. I could sleep right here," she said while dropping her head back on the cushion behind her.

She turned her face toward me and picked up the topic we had started. "So can you explain what 'yes and no' means regarding my question about always wanting to teach? Like, when did you decide that's what you wanted to do? Did you have any other jobs before this one?"

I went through a brief accounting of my own university experience and how my parents were very unhappy with me when I changed my major two times in four years.

"Do you have a close relationship with your parents?" the beautiful woman asked between heavy-lidded blinks. She'd be sleeping in the next ten minutes. Maybe less.

"Probably to a normal degree. My father passed away a few years ago, so my mother is alone in the Midwest where I grew up. I've tried to get her to move out here so I could do a better job keeping an eye on her, but she won't do it." I thought about what I was saying and added, "Eventually she may have to whether she wants to or not. My life and career are here. When she gets to a point that she can't care for herself, being in Nebraska won't help either of us."

"Nebraska?" she repeated with wide eyes. "I don't think I've ever met anyone from that state. Tell me what it was like growing up there. Was your father a farmer?"

The comment made me chuckle. "There are other career paths besides farming in the state. He sold insurance. Mostly to farmers."

She poked a finger into my side, and we both laughed. I couldn't pass up the opportunity to touch her, though, and since she was bold enough to touch my body, I instantly wanted more of the physical contact.

I scooped her hand into mine and simply entwined our fingers. Even her hands were pretty. Soft and delicate, her slim fingers were tipped with freshly manicured nails. They fit so perfectly with mine, and I must have stared down where we were joined for longer than I should have, because I felt her grow tense.

"What's wrong?" she asked with an edge of alarm lacing her tone.

"Nothing." I smiled, but based on her raised single brow, she wasn't buying it. Fine, I could be a little more vulnerable here. Maybe if we laid our feelings out on the table, we could stop wasting time dancing around them and start enjoying each other fully.

"I want to keep touching you. I want you to touch me. I've been fantasizing about you since the first day in class, and I feel like I'm going to suddenly wake up from a really cruel but fantastic dream."

From behind her hand, she stifled another yawn. I had to pull myself back by the collar and be a gentleman here. The reason I insisted she come to my house was so I could take care of her and her injured arm. Forcing her to stay awake now wasn't in accordance with that plan at all. My dick wouldn't be happy, but it was the right thing to do.

"Baby, let's get you tucked in for the night before I'm carrying you to bed. Not that I'd mind doing that. Believe me."

Her smile was slow and languid and as seductive as I'd seen on her face. Leading her slowly down the hall, I was battling every urge not to pin her against the wall and kiss her.

"I can just sleep on the couch, really. You don't have to go through all this trouble," she protested when I guided her to sit on the guest room bed while I hurried off to get her something to sleep in.

For some reason, that simple task brought me up short. I stood in front of my chest of drawers, staring into the one that held all my T-shirts. What the hell was I doing here? Was I jeopardizing everything I worked so hard and so long for in the name of physical gratification? How bad would this information go over with the university's board of trustees?

I swiped a shirt off the top of the stack in my drawer, and it made sense why my mind took that momentary detour. The school's crest was emblazoned on the front and must have sparked the tangent in my brain. My body overrode any thoughts of putting the brakes on with the little doll in my guest room, though.

Maye was lying on her side, her long, full mane cascading across both pillows. Her eyes were closed and her breathing soft, but I was sure she didn't want to sleep in her clothes. She didn't have anything else with her and would have to wear them again in the morning. I needed to wake her but hated doing it.

Kneeling beside the bed, I laid my shirt on the mattress and just stared at her. She was the most beautiful woman I'd ever seen. Her features were relaxed from the pain reliever and sleep, and if I had been any good at it, I'd draw or paint her there in that pose. She was a goddess. Simply perfect in every way.

Her skin was flawless and soft, and without thinking more about it, I stroked my fingers across her forehead and along her cheekbone. At my touch, her mouth curved into a sleepy smile. Before saying anything, I stroked some stray hair back from her neck and finger-combed it into the mass on the pillow.

Voice at a whisper, I told her, "I got you something to

sleep in."

Without opening her eyes, she muttered, "Okay, thank you."

I stood from my kneeling position and offered, "Let me help you sit up and get your clothes off."

Her eyes popped open at my suggestion, and I grinned, trying to interpret the expression. Was she nervous? How experienced was she? Did I have the strength to see her bare skin and not mount her?

She was fully awake now and sat up. "I'm sure I can manage myself. You must be tired too. Please, don't let me keep you from going to bed yourself."

Little did she know, I had every intention of sleeping in this bed with her. At least that was my plan. If she protested, I'd go to my own room. Wouldn't be happy about it, but I would do it. It sucked always being the good guy. I had to tell myself that being patient would be worth it in the long run. There was no sense in destroying the woman's trust because I was so turned on by her.

I smiled at her careful protest and asked, "Do you argue about everything? Or only when someone is trying to help you?" With one knee on the mattress, I leaned over her. Those incredibly deep, intelligent blue eyes followed my place above her, so I explained, "I'm going to help you sit up so you don't put pressure on your arm."

"Oh," she said in a breathy exhale that almost knocked me dead. She really had no idea how alluring she was. If she did, she was an expert actress. "Okay."

With my arms beneath her shoulders, I cradled her torso against my chest and rocked us both until she was sitting. "There. Better, right?"

"Yes, thank you. How did you do that?" The wonder in her voice filled my male pride cup right to the rim.

"When my father was dying, I helped my mother care for him. The nurses taught us a lot of little tricks that made caregiving in the home easier."

Maye touched my arm with her delicate hand until I asked, "What?"

"I'm sorry about your dad. I'm sorry if it made you sad... remembering just then."

"No, I'm not sad, baby. Years have gone by now."

She shook her head. "Just because time has passed doesn't make a loss less profound."

"You're right. There are days I pick up my phone to call him." I paused for a second and grinned. "Stupid, right? I mean, I know he's gone. But we used to be pretty close. I shared all my good and bad days with him. Those are usually the times it still hits me."

"That's so sweet. I wish I could've met him. Seen your friendship with him."

I knew she wasn't just offering a societal nicety. She truly meant what she'd said.

"He would've liked you," I said with a smile before adding more. "He would say you're too young for me, but yeah..." My smile grew bigger. "He would've liked you."

Before the air got too heavy with dead-people talk, I said, "It's perfect that you have a button-down on. I think it will make this easier." I paused before reaching out to unbutton her blouse.

Her whole body tensed, and I dropped my hands.

"What is it?" she asked, studying me closely.

"You are very astute, you know that? You see much more

than most people see."

She looked bashful before admitting, "You know...you aren't the only one who watched someone all semester."

That was her shy way of telling me she'd been interested in me too for much longer than this week. I didn't think it would serve anyone's confidence to tell her there had been times I thought she was watching me with a different kind of interest than the other students. I had always chalked it up to my wishful thinking.

"So I feel like I know you, on some sort of level, I guess," she added. "But why did you abort your mission here?" She looked down at the buttons on her shirt, then met my attentive gaze.

"Your whole body stiffened when I reached to get started, so I paused. I don't want to do anything you don't want. And I'm trying to be gentlemanly here. Even though my guy brain is egging me on in the opposite direction."

My honesty coaxed that gentle smile I was quickly getting addicted to. I was starting to think there wasn't anything I wouldn't do to bring one of those out.

"No. It wasn't your touch that made me tense. Honestly." I was treated to a fantastic eye roll, and I was reminded how young she was.

It still didn't make me want to abort this task.

"The more I'm thinking about having to do this," she continued, "the more I'm thinking I should just sleep in my clothes. It's really going to hurt maneuvering out of the sleeve."

"You don't have other clothes here. I didn't think you'd want to spend a whole day tomorrow in clothes you slept in. I can start some laundry once we get these things off."

"I can just get up earlier and go home before coming into

the office tomorrow. Well, heck, I don't even know what time it is. Maybe it's today already." She rubbed the tension expressed across her forehead.

It wasn't a terrible option, so I figured I'd leave the decision to her without any more coercing from me. Yes, I really wanted to see her without clothes on. Not denying that. But again, I was really trying to avoid spooking her.

"You tell me what you want to do, baby, and I'll do it."

Her shy smile made another appearance, and I couldn't stop myself from leaning closer and kissing her. She had the most seductive, pouty lips, and I was completely obsessed with them. Maye Farsey was a true knockout, but that mouth was my favorite feature of them all.

"What is this smile about?" I asked with my lips still pressed to hers.

"What?" She pulled back a little. "Oh, nothing. It's silly."

I shifted back a bit. "Nothing that comes from this incredible, creative mind could be considered silly, young lady." I didn't miss her barely there wince at that term, and I wanted to kick myself for using it. I muttered a quick "Sorry" but was still curious about that smile. If I knew what brought it out, I'd keep doing whatever I was doing to cause it.

"I like that." She shrugged, and now I was truly confused.

"The kiss?" I asked hopefully and closed the gap between us to give her another one.

"No." She laughed, low and throaty. "That's not what I meant. Though I do enjoy those too."

"What, then? And I will kiss you every chance I can get."

She kept her eyes down while tracing the pattern on the bedspread with her index finger. Whatever she was about to admit made her shy.

As though she decided to just go for it, with a shrug she said, "I like when you call me baby. I don't know why." She shrugged again. "It's so sweet. There's a side to you I didn't know existed before. I guess with the evening's events, I'm glad I get a chance to see it." She studied my reaction and added, "I don't know if any of that makes sense. I'm so tired, I feel like I'm babbling."

"I'm glad you like it when I call you that. It's not a conscious decision. It just comes out. As far as the different side of my personality you're seeing"—I paused and gave her a playfully stern look—"I'm not so sure about all that."

She pushed my leg with her uninjured hand. "You know what I mean. I'm glad that tonight, while maybe I need a little more tenderness than you normally show, you're being so sweet. So compassionate."

"I don't think I'll ever forgive myself for you getting hurt. If I hadn't frightened you, you wouldn't have run off. But when I saw that boy with his hands on you—"

"You didn't frighten me. Honestly. You didn't. I've always had the flight instinct way stronger than fight." Quietly, she added, "It can really be a character flaw in certain circumstances, though."

After tilting my head a bit, I asked, "How do you mean?"

"Well, when I should be sticking up for myself or demanding justice for someone I care about, what good is running away?"

"Okay, true enough. But it's not always helpful to be confrontational. Things don't get solved with aggression. Not truly fixed, anyway. In fact, a lot of times, arguing about a topic either creates more dissension or takes you off the point you want to make."

Maye slipped off the bed and stood.

I watched her quizzically. Did everything I just say make her so uncomfortable that she wanted to leave? How could that be? I must have had a panicked look on my face, because she touched my arm to reassure me.

"I just need to use the bathroom before I fall asleep. But then we definitely need to get some shut-eye, or neither one of us will be of any use in the office tomorrow."

"Here, let me show you where the bathroom is. Can you manage yourself?"

She gave me a look like *Don't even think about it, man,* and I chuckled. "Well, I'll be here if you get into a bind in there. Okay?"

"Thank you. For everything," she said as we walked down the hall. "You've been amazing, and I'm glad I came back here with you."

"Okay, right here." I motioned with my arm to the open bathroom door. I quickly reached in and flipped on the light for her and stood back.

While she used the bathroom, I scurried back to the bedroom and pulled down the bedspread and sheet. She could slip right in when she came back, and I planned on tucking her in and heeding her wise advice. As difficult as it would be, we both needed sleep.

The next morning, Maye was up before me. I fell asleep on top of the covers alongside her in the guest room. I watched her sleep for most of the night, so I felt like a zombie when I heard her moving around the room.

"What are you doing?" I asked sleepily. Keeping my eyes open long enough to track her activity was more than I could accomplish. "How's the arm?" I asked the second I was awake enough to gather my thoughts.

"It's okay. Not as bad as last night, thankfully," she said through that perfected, albeit manufactured, smile. "Whatever you gave me was good stuff, though. I was sure I wouldn't be able to sleep because of it. But the minute I was horizontal, I was out cold. I don't think I moved all night."

I wanted to say, *You didn't, trust me,* but thought better about it, realizing how creepy that would appear. So instead, I matched her forced smile with one of my own.

"I'm so glad. Are you going to have it looked at today? I'd understand completely if you can't come in first thing."

"I thought I'd play it by ear. I need to get home and shower and regroup a little. I'll be able to assess how swollen it is and what kind of range I have after that. At least that's the game plan I've come up with."

"How long have you been up?" I asked. She was very chipper already for a woman with only a handful of hours of sleep. Mentally, I kicked myself. She was young. Young people were so much more resilient on a reduced sleep schedule.

"Not long at all. Less than an hour. I've called for a ride. I saw your address on some mail on the kitchen island. I hope that's okay?"

"Of course," I said, finally sitting up. She was definitely in a hurry to leave, and I debated calling her on it or just letting her go. "Have you had coffee? I can make some," I offered while standing and straightening the bedding.

I was so used to being alone, I didn't think twice about the morning erection Maye couldn't take her curious blue eyes from.

"Oh, sorry," I said, trying to rearrange things in my sleep pants. It was no use. There'd be no hiding it until it calmed itself down.

Her gaze darted from my crotch to my face and back again. Finally, in a voice so husky it nearly broke me, she said, "All good. Biology is biology, right?"

"Right," I mumbled as we walked down the hall toward the front door.

She was studying her phone screen like most girls her age did, and it was unusual. I rarely saw the woman use her phone, which was so refreshing. When she announced, "Oh! Looks like my ride is here," and looked up, it was to find me staring at her.

"Thank you for everything, Andrew. I guess I'll see you today sometime?" she said as I disarmed my security system and opened the door for her.

"Yes. If you decide to have it looked at by a doctor, please just let me know so I don't think you're lying in a ditch somewhere."

"Of course! Ummm, okay." She stalled on the front step, looking more awkward than I'd seen a woman the morning after.

I leaned closer and pecked her cheek. Since she was rushing off, I didn't have time to brush yet. No way would I kiss her the way I wanted to.

But the chaste farewell seemed to make her uneasiness worse. She hurried off down the walk to the waiting vehicle so haphazardly, I thought she'd take another spill. I stood there watching the little hybrid vehicle until it disappeared around the first bend.

My gut was in knots. I would've bet money that was the first and last time I'd see her leave my house.

CHAPTER TEN

MAYE

I should've expected the traffic mess I sat in when leaving Andrew's house. It took three times longer than it should've to get home to Brentwood. By the time I opened the front door, my dad was already gone for the day, and my mom was busy cleaning up the kitchen from his breakfast.

"Maye? Is that you?" she called over her shoulder while elbow deep in the dishwater's suds.

"Hey, Mom. Yeah, it's me."

"You've been out and about early this morning," she said, and there was no way I'd be able to escape to my room.

Did I admit I was just getting home, or play along with her version of my morning's activities?

"Actually, I'm just coming home. But I need to get showered and off to school. I don't want Professor Chaplin to be upset."

Well, that did it. Even though telling the truth was always the better plan with either of my parents, this behavior would have been expected more from my older sister, Agatha, when she lived at home, or even my twin.

My mom confirmed my thought when she commented, "This isn't like you. Everything okay, dear?" She came to where the kitchen became the great room and wiped her hands on the dish towel that was flung over one shoulder.

"Yes, fine. Just had a late night, and it made more sense to stay instead of getting a ride. Shepperd had the car." As I explained my whereabouts, she was eagle-eyeing my arm. Maybe the way I was holding it against my chest out of habit now, or the way the thing was still swollen to twice its normal size, but she didn't like what she saw.

"Maye Louise! What happened?" She rushed toward me, and I physically recoiled from her approach. The damn thing was throbbing like nobody's business, and the last thing I wanted was her touching it.

"I fell. It's fine, Mom. Seriously. I'm just going to shower and—"

"No way, young lady. That needs to be looked at. It's huge!" That was typical Lisa Farsey—stater of the obvious.

"Whether I go to the doctor or school, I need a shower. Please. Just let me freshen up, and we can decide what to do."

"Fine. But I'm calling Dr. Miller while you shower. Hopefully, they can fit you in."

"There's no point going to his office, Mom. He's just going to send me for an X-ray. If we do anything, we may as well go straight to urgent care, and they can x-ray it right there in their building." I'd given this plenty of thought already, and that was the best plan.

"Okay, you have a point. I'll drive you. I'll cancel my Pilates class this morning. Sound like a plan?"

I sagged with relief and frustration at the same time. I hated to put anyone out, and I knew she coveted that time at her fitness class. Guilt already niggled at me that she would miss today's session.

"No, Mom. We can go later. So you won't have to miss

class," I offered. "It barely hurts."

Lies, lies, lies.

She gave the idea consideration but snapped out of her moment of selfishness and insisted we go as soon as I showered. I knew I shouldn't think that about the same woman who devoted her entire life to raising my sisters and me. But an injured or sick child in this house never got the attention she deserved. Or at least what we thought we should get.

It was a strange sticking point for not just me but for all my siblings. We talked about it on numerous occasions, and we all harbored the same resentment about it. When we were children and got the flu or whatever was going around school, we were told to tough it out. My parents firmly believed our immune systems were stronger because we didn't interfere with antibiotics. While I was sure there was some logic to the theory, there were plenty of times it seemed like unnecessary suffering.

"Do you need help? How are you going to undress?" she asked when she refocused on me and not her disrupted routine.

"I'll manage. I'll be quick. No way I'm washing my hair today with one arm. It will just have to be a bun day," I called back to her as I headed toward my room. "Just give me twenty minutes."

"Okay, honey. Holler if you need help."

By the time I had my clothes off and stood beneath the shower spray, I was in tears. The damn arm really hurt, and since I'd been keeping it immobilized, it was so much more painful when I did move it. If the damn thing wasn't broken, I'd be shocked.

Seven hours, five X-rays, two orthopedic consultations, and one blue fiberglass cast later, I collapsed utterly exhausted onto my bed. That was one of the longest, most painful days I could remember.

Of course, I texted Andrew throughout the process—at his insistence, to let him know what was happening. The end result was a broken ulna and a terribly uncomfortable cast up to my armpit.

Unreal. That was the only word that could summarize it. In the interminable wait between various steps in the process, I ended up telling my mother what actually happened. I wished I'd skipped over the part about Joel manhandling me, because she would surely tell my dad what had happened. Though, if he beat the boy's ass for it, it only served him right.

If he had just respected my dismissal the first time. Or hell, the second or third time, even, none of this would've happened. I definitely painted Andrew as the hero in the situation because in my memory, that's what he had been. Who knows how unhinged Joel would've become had he not stepped in. For that, I would always be thankful.

All the stuff that happened after that? Well—jury was still out on the soundness of those decisions. At least I didn't sleep with the man or anything like that. Then I'd have a mountain of what-ifs plaguing me right now instead of the handful.

Obviously, I was excused from missing the day at school with him. He told me to take the rest of the week off—to recover. Now that I was home, enormous arm resting on a pile of pillows beside me, I had some head time to really worry about the whole situation.

Was he telling me to stay home because he was uncomfortable around me now? Did he ever date any of his other students or interns? Was I just another nubile notch in his bedpost? My rational mind said he was sincere with everything he said and did the night before. The jaded version, admittedly heavily influenced by my twin, had me doubting every single detail as I replayed the night back in my memory.

The doctor at the hospital had prescribed a mild pain reliever, and when there was a soft knock on our bedroom door, I hoped it was my mom, back from the pharmacy with the medication.

"Maye, darling? You awake, sweetie?" Her alto voice was easy to discern through the closed panel.

"Yeah, Mom. Come on in," I called from the nest of pillows.

"Honey, you have a visitor. Are you up for some company?"

"Oh, Mom, I don't think so. Were you able to get that prescription?" I really just wanted to get some relief from the throbbing pain and go to sleep.

"I was just heading to the pharmacy now. Are you sure you want me to tell him no? He said he's your professor—"

My voice shot up into cartoon character range. "Andrew is here? Seriously?"

Her raised brow pointed out my slip, but I didn't give her look any attention. It wasn't unheard of for professors to permit students to use their first names in class. If I acted guilty, she'd assume I was.

"So you do want me to show him in?" she clarified while I tried to improve my ragged appearance.

I finger-combed the hair that had escaped the low braid my mom styled this morning. Taking quick stock of what I mindlessly threw on after we got home, I decided it would have to do because I wasn't changing again. It took fifteen minutes the first time, and I planned on spending the next three days in the same outfit if I could.

My mother cleared her throat in the doorway, and I realized in my panic and excitement, I hadn't answered her.

"Yes, please, Mom, if you don't mind? And thank you for going to the pharmacy. It really hurts."

"All right, honey. I'm sorry it's taken me this long. You know how your father likes his dinner at the same time. Then I had to clean up the dishes, and—"

"Thanks, Mom." I had to cut her off before she continued listing the myriad chores she did in a day. Guilt upon guilt upon guilt. Whether she knew she was doing it or not, the jury was still out.

In a few minutes, she appeared at my room again with a very dignified but fidgeting Professor Chaplin behind her. I had straightened the covers on my bed the best I could accomplish with one arm and sat back against a stack of pillows. My cast looked like a bright-blue beacon in the middle of my snowy-white bedding.

"Maye." He sighed. It was like just seeing me calmed his entire body.

"Hi," I said, suddenly feeling very shy. It was awkward that this man was seeing me in my childhood bedroom, surrounded by all the treasures I'd accumulated through my youth. Never in a million years would I have imagined the two of us being here.

My mom hovered in the hall just outside the door until I cleared my throat and thanked her for showing my guest to my room.

"Honey, just holler if you need anything, okay? Clemson should be home from practice soon, and Dad is watching TV. I'll be back in no time with your medication."

If I were on my feet, I would've shoved her down the hall

to get her moving in the right direction.

"Thanks, Mom. I really appreciate everything you've done today." Even though she was making the scene more awkward at the moment, I couldn't have gotten through the day without her. Apparently, there were always going to be days when I just needed my mom, no matter how old I was.

Andrew watched her until she was out of sight, then fixed his intense stare on me. He took no more than three strides to dissolve the distance between us and sat on the edge of my bed alongside my hip.

"How are you feeling?" His voice was so deep and sincere, I felt my lower abdomen clench.

My first attempt at speech came out raspier than I thought possible. I swallowed and tried again. "I'm fine. Still hurts, but she's picking something up so I can sleep." I motioned to the doorway with my chin to indicate my mother.

He scooped up my left hand in his, and I studied how his body was so much larger than mine. After the day I had, I was feeling very vulnerable and emotional. Just his simple gesture flooded my eyes with unshed tears, and I did everything I knew to choke them back. Of course, he didn't miss my silly reaction to his simple gesture.

"Hey, what's all this? I wish I had known you were suffering. I would've brought more pain relievers with me." He gave me a cautious look before saying, "Please don't take this the wrong way, but why is she just going to the pharmacy now? You've been home from the hospital for hours, and I can see how much pain you're in just by the look on your face." His scowl grew in intensity the more he spoke. "I would think that would have been the priority, no?"

"It's fine," I began, but he widened his eyes, and I stopped speaking midsentence.

"It's not fine. You're not fine. You should've had that relief hours ago. If I had known it was just sitting there waiting to be picked up, I could've done it for you. This whole goddamn mess is my fault in the first place."

And even though he muttered that last part, I was already shaking my head in denial before I could formulate my response. "Andrew, please stop saying that. This was not your fault." I squeezed his hand after saying that so he would look at me. He had been unusually uncomfortable while I exonerated him.

We needed a topic change. "Thank you for coming to see me. It was very unexpected."

"I knew if I called and asked, you would have said no, so I took a chance and just came over. I needed to see with my own eyes that you were okay."

"How do you already know me so well? I have a very thick vein of guilt that runs through my psyche. Whenever anyone does anything for me that I think is putting them out, I get a really bad case of the guilts."

He leaned closer and kissed the tip of my nose. The gesture was so sweet, but what I really wanted was to kiss him like I experienced last night.

"I think I'm going to make it my personal mission to break you of that habit," he said, his sly, playful grin making him look boyishly handsome.

"Is that right?" I teased back and chased his mouth for another peck. If that's all I could have, I'd take it. But he deepened the kiss I instigated, and after a minute of our tongues stabbing and dueling, a low groan vibrated out of him and straight into me.

We pulled apart, and I suspected my facial expression mirrored his. He had to know how badly I didn't want to stop.

"If you close and lock the door, you could lie with me?" I suggested the idea with the lilt of a question because I wasn't sure how he'd react. I didn't want to feel embarrassed if he shot me down.

"I think you need your rest, baby. Not your horny professor groping you through your pj's." He cushioned the rejection with a wink, and if I were wearing panties beneath my sleep shorts, they would've melted right off.

"I don't know..." I drew out playfully. "I could make a case for that."

"Oh, the day will come—if I have a say in the matter," he assured. "So are you going to let people deface this thing?" He motioned to my cast, changing the subject.

I plastered on a masterful pout, and he chuckled.

"Why? Do you want to be the first to write your name on it?"

"Honestly, I'd like my name to be the only one on it." He made the comment so nonchalantly, I thought maybe I misunderstood what he said.

Luckily, he saved me from having to come up with a response to his unexpected possessive comment by once more changing the subject altogether.

"So how long in the cast? Will you need physical therapy when it comes off?"

"The doctor said six to eight weeks in the cast, which is basically the entire summer." I pouted again in case he didn't pick up my opinion on that tidbit from my tone. "He said we have to play it by ear when the cast comes off. If I have good range of motion after the bone heals, maybe not. Since I'm young and otherwise healthy, it should heal just fine. I was lucky because it is a pretty clean fracture."

He grew very solemn then and apologized again. "I'm so sorry."

"Look. If you apologize one more time, I'm going to kick you out of here and not show up to school tomorrow." Yes, my threat was empty, but he had to stop taking ownership for my clumsiness.

"Hmmm." He made the noise dark and sexy somehow. "Who knew you were so bossy under this sweet good-girl exterior?"

"Good girl, huh?" I tried to laugh, but it sounded as awkward as me refuting that was the vibe I put off.

Andrew raised a brow skeptically. "Are you telling me you're really a bad, bad girl under all this pretty fluff?" He fingered the end of my braid, and even that slight touch sent thrills through my whole body.

He leaned closer to kiss me again, but there was a loud knock on the doorframe. I had completely forgotten the door was still wide open.

"Hey there... Whoa..." my twin clipped as she strode across the room. "Don't mind me. I just need to grab my laptop, and I'll be out of the way."

I let out a huge sigh of relief that it had been her and not one of my parents.

"Hey, Shep!" I said, excited to see her. It had been days, and I missed her. I was so anxious to catch her up with what had happened between my professor and me. Of course, I couldn't do that with the man sitting on the edge of my bed, but the minute he left, I'd tell her everything.

In the meantime, I made some introductions. "Andrew,

this is my sister, Shepperd. Shep, this is my...my ummm..."
Okay, so I hadn't thought this through. At all.

While I fumbled and stammered about what to call him, he stood and crossed the room to offer a friendly hand to my twin.

"Andrew Chaplin. How are you?" he said without missing a beat.

With a weary expression, Shepperd took his hand and mumbled some sort of greeting. She was eyeballing the guy up and down, though, and like always, I felt compelled to interject.

"How was your day? I haven't seen you since, what? The day before yesterday?"

Rather than answer the question I asked, she bugged her eyes out when she got a view of the bright-blue cast.

"Whooaaa, Mayday. What the hell happened? Are you okay?"

Before she could rein it back in, her natural concern for me shone through. Just hearing her distress made my heart swell, and my smile couldn't be contained. It probably outwardly looked like an odd reaction to her worry, but we all had become too accustomed to the bitter version of her lately, and it was a nice surprise to see the caring, compassionate sister I grew up with.

"Just a fracture. Nothing that a little time won't heal," I said dismissively. Out of the corner of my eye, I saw Andrew wince at my remark.

Shepperd wasn't nearly as subtle, though. She shook her head in obvious disappointment.

"What?" I asked in a mixture of frustration and a whine. It had been the longest day, and I just wanted someone to cut me some slack.

"Only you, Maye Louise."

I cringed at the use of my old-fashioned middle name and rewarded her with an eye roll. "You had to use that name, didn't you?"

Her spreading grin matched mine. "You deserve it when you act so dumb."

"Pardon?" I asked incredulously. "Dumb?"

"Yes. Dumb as dirt. Who the hell breaks their arm and says words like just and little?"

"I just don't like when people make a fuss over me. You know that." I probably said that more for Andrew's benefit than my sibling's. The girl knew me better than anyone and didn't need my reminding her of my character.

But then she turned on a dime as though it had just struck her who the man in the room with us was.

She looked at him from head to toe. "You're the teacher?"

He didn't back down an inch, even with her acidic tone. I had no idea what caused the sudden mood switch, but instinctually, I wanted to interfere.

So I answered before Andrew could. "Yes, this is Professor Chaplin. He's mentoring me through the summer internship. He was there yesterday when I fell and stopped by to see how I was doing." I rushed the whole explanation out in one breath and begged her with every twin wavelength we shared to just leave it at that.

"Interesting," she said with a tone so loaded with innuendo, you'd have to be dense to miss it.

"Indeed it is," Andrew answered, and I caught the mischievous grin he tried to conceal with a forced cough.

"Well, I really just needed to grab my computer. I have to do some extra credit for chemistry, or I'm not going to pass."

"Oh noooo," I commiserated. "Do you need some help?"

"Weren't you going to get some rest?" Andrew interjected, and Shepperd and I both shot him stay-out-of-it glares.

"Okay. That was wild." With a little head shake and a chuckle, he explained, "When you both gave me the exact same evil eye at the same exact time. Not going to lie, that was trippy."

Shepperd looked at me and mouthed *trippy?*, and I burst out laughing. Poor Andrew missed the interaction, so he was left out of our laughing fit.

"Nice to meet you," she called over her shoulder, and praise to my twin, closed the door to our shared room on her way out.

Andrew stalked back to the bed and loomed over me while he asked, "What's so funny, Ms. Farsey?"

Instantly my throat went bone-dry, and I tried to swallow the ball of lust his tone created. Reaching out with my uninjured arm, I grabbed the man by the front of his dress shirt and pulled him to my mouth.

I'd show him just how not nice I could be.

CHAPTER ELEVEN

ANDREW

And that's how I ended up lying on top of Maye in her childhood bedroom. Under the same roof with her parents and siblings. It would've taken an earthquake equal to The Big One or some other catastrophic event to have made me stop, too.

I was careful not to jostle her casted injury as I settled my weight between her bare legs. So many times, I'd fantasized about those long, toned legs around my hips or waist while I slammed into her. My God, the real thing was unbelievably better than I'd imagined.

"Fuck me, baby. You are so sweet, so perfect," I praised between devouring her. I made a path of intentionally wet kisses across her jaw to behind her ear and then continued down her long, graceful swan's neck. She was so fucking beautiful, it caused a pain deep in my soul. My cock was thick and insistent, and I gave a cautious rock against her warm center.

Maye moaned in pleasure, so I repeated the motion while watching her expression. She had her head tipped back in the downy pile of pillows, her blond hair fighting to free itself from the braid she had confined it to. The mass of thick, golden strands looked like silk spread across the ultra-white bedding, and all I could think of were cherubs with sweet apple cheeks and pouty bow-shaped mouths.

The things I wanted to do to that mouth would make her blush that perfect hue of fuchsia she turned when embarrassed. I vowed to eliminate any trace of unease and train her body to crave mine like any other basic need.

Between kisses, she silently begged me with a glassy, needy stare.

"What is it? What do you need?" I encouraged before diving back down to her throat to nip at the thin skin there.

"Oh my—" she stuttered from the sharp bite. "Shit, that feels so good."

"Your skin tastes divine. I knew it would." I muttered that last part under my breath but felt the skin of her cheek pull tighter as she smiled. She heard how enraptured I was with her physically and loved it.

With her delicate fingers, she began tugging at the buttons on the front of my shirt, and my better sense finally kicked in. If I felt her body beneath me, skin to skin, I wouldn't be able to stop until I was inside her. Regardless of her encouragement, I refused to do that with her family in the house.

I had to draw the line somewhere, and the foolishness of the thought made me laugh. Right in the middle of a searing kiss.

Maye widened her eyes and stared up at me. "You're laughing? Did I do something?"

I quickly silenced her by pressing my lips to hers, but I didn't open when she tried to find her way back inside my mouth.

"Oh, you've done plenty of things. But we need to stop, or there will be no turning back. I'm already going to hell for doing any of this in the first place, but I won't fuck you with your dad in the next room." I shook my head slowly even though I was still grinning. "No way."

"But—but it feels so good. You feel so good. I don't want to stop. Please—"

By some divine intervention or mother's intuition, or hell—who knows what, because my brain was so starved of blood because it was all supplying my hard-on—there was a quick, firm knock on the closed door, causing me to scurry off the bed and halfway across the room.

For Christ's sake, I was acting like a teenager.

We weren't going to fool anyone, though. Maye's full lips were red and well kissed, and we were both breathing hard enough to make our chests rise and fall.

The knock came again, this time accompanied by her mother's raspy voice.

Well, now I knew where Maye got the vocal gift from. And from what I'd heard from her twin, both girls took after their mom.

"Maye? Darling, I have your prescription. Can I come in?"

Maye sat up taller, and I rushed back to the bedside to help straighten the pillows and blankets across her lap. My erection was quickly deflating, and by the time the woman opened the door, I hoped it wasn't noticeable.

I scooped up the nearest book from what looked like a shared desk and held it at a particular angle to hide any remaining proof of what I was just doing with her daughter. I didn't miss the grin on my obsession's face when she figured out what I was up to, either.

"Oh, honey." Lisa Farsey beelined to her daughter's bedside. "I'm wondering if you have a fever." She felt Maye's forehead with her flat palm and said, "You're really flushed."

Maye ducked out of the way and said, "I'm fine. I had too many blankets on. That's all." She reached for the bag and thanked her mom again. "I'm just going to get this on board and get to bed. It's been a long day."

"That's my cue to get going," I said, hoping her mother would leave us to say goodbye.

"Okay, dear. Just holler if you need anything. It was very nice to meet you," she directed my way with a kind smile.

"Likewise," I said as the woman bustled out of the room. When she was gone, I sat on the edge of the bed again, but this time, I kept my hands to myself.

"Listen," I said to Maye. "I don't want you to feel like you have to be back at school tomorrow. Take a few days off to rest and recover a bit. Let your body start healing."

Disappointment washed over her face. "I'll go crazy lying around here for more than a day. I'm sure I'll be fine."

A growl worked up my throat, and I gave her a stern look. I was coming to despise the *I'll be fine* three-word combo. Especially coming from Maye's lips.

"Well, you certainly won't be expected, so you make the call. I'll check in with you. If that's okay, I mean, sometime tomorrow to see how you're doing." Yes, I was being a bit protective, but I'd already witnessed her denial of her own well-being. If she wouldn't care for herself properly, I'd do it for her.

She treated me to that soft smile I adored and admitted quietly, "I'd like that." Then, as if jolted by a current, she lit up with an idea. "Maybe there's something I can work on from here? I can continue researching opportunities from those websites."

I gave her a stern expression. "I don't want you overdoing it. It will be hard to type, and I'm sure your doctor told you to keep that thing elevated for a few days." I watched her carefully for her reaction to my suspicion because I would almost bet she was about to say she was fine again. Maybe by reminding her of the medical professional's advice, she'd give herself permission to take some time off.

At her crestfallen face, I assured her, "It's only a few days, baby. We're not going to fall behind. We can always put in some after-office hours when you're up to it again." I waggled my brows so she'd understand my thinking. This actually provided a perfect excuse to see her in private again.

"Good idea." She grinned but then sagged with resignation. "All right, fine," she relented. "I'll rest as long as I can. But seriously, I hate lying around. I'm not very good at relaxing."

Standing, I leaned down and kissed her forehead. "I'll talk to you tomorrow. Get some sleep."

Driving home with a relentless smile, I replayed the evening over and over. I could smell the divine young woman on my clothes, and with the insistence of my erection since getting in the car, I knew I'd be jerking off to her memory before I'd get a wink of sleep.

The next two days dragged by. I texted with Maye off and on and had to stop myself from coming on too strong or calling her. But all bets were off by day three, and even though we were about to head into the weekend, I knew I'd go nuts if I didn't see her soon.

Ms. Donnio poked her head in my doorway about an hour before quitting time.

"Andrew... Hey there," she purred in an attempt at being seductive. Or at least that was my guess, because the whole routine did nothing but repulse me. My colleague was the exact opposite of Maye on so many levels, I couldn't imagine even talking to her longer than necessary.

"Hello," I said. At least I could be polite.

"A bunch of us are going to happy hour down at G-Street. Feel like going?"

G-Street was a local bar just a few blocks away from campus. The vibe inside the joint was upscale enough to keep the students from frequenting the place and affordable enough that a family could have a decent meal there.

I didn't have plans for the weekend—at all—and was tempted to join them. I usually had to force myself to socialize with workmates but did so on occasion to not be lumped into the category with the staff that the others whispered about.

"Maybe a drink or two." I cringed at the way her face lit up. "When are you all going? I might stop by," I added, hoping I planted enough opportunity to also not show up.

"Straight from here. I can give you a lift if you really want to cut loose."

I frowned despite how amiable I was trying to be. "That's nice of you, but I'm really tired. If I go, it will just be to say hi. Thanks, though."

She put on a ridiculous, dramatic display of disappointment before her attention was caught by someone else in the hallway, and she snapped out of her nonsense.

As she was closing my door, she said, "See you there," and was gone.

As she spoke to her new victim in the corridor, I could hear the low murmuring of voices but couldn't discern what they were actually saying. My door opened again after a few minutes, and I looked up with visible impatience after logging off my school computer.

I expected to see Rebecca in the entrance, so I was completely surprised to see that idiot that kept coming around to see Maye.

Joe, maybe?

After whipping off the glasses I wore for lengthy sessions in front of a computer, I dropped the heavy frames on my desk with a *thud*.

"Can I help you?" I asked the kid.

The little shit had the nerve to scowl my way before sneering, "I'm looking for Maye. Not that it's your business."

"Well, see, that's where you're wrong. This"—I swept my arm wide between us—"is my office. So you're already getting off to a really shaky start walking in here with that giant chip on your shoulder."

"Is she here or not?" he asked with absolutely no course correction.

"Not."

He must not have expected that answer, because he responded like a petulant child in a playground argument.

"Where is she?"

In my mind, I wanted to match his immature mien and say something like *That's for me to know and you to find out*, but in reality, I grinned. Having the upper hand was so sweet, and I'd be damned if I'd take much more from the guy.

Slowly, I rose from my seat, and the notion of protecting Maye from this guy, in any way thinkable, made me feel at least six inches taller.

The coward looked over his shoulder to get a quick reference point on the door's location. Guessing in case he had to run away again like last time we met.

"You know, my dad's an attorney."

I laughed at his comment. "Is there a reason you're listing your father's résumé?"

He continued with his stupid, pointless blustering. "I've seen the way you look at her. How old are you, anyway? Like fifty?" He said the number through a twisted sneer, and I wanted to punch his entitled, clueless lights out.

"Time to go, junior." I took two steps in his direction, and the coward skittered back toward the door. "I'm not sure what your problem is exactly, but don't come around here again, or I'll report you to the dean. From what I've seen and heard, Ms. Farsey has told you to leave her alone several times. If Daddy Dearest is a lawyer, you might want to hire him for when you're charged with stalking."

"She's my girlfriend, dumbass."

"It's my understanding she dumped you."

"No. We're just going through a rough spot. That's why I wanted to see her today. It's our anniversary, and, well, I know she's probably missing me. I wanted to give her another chance."

I couldn't hold back my chuckle. Shaking my head, I said to the kid, "Look. Spare whatever dignity you have left and go home. Like I said, she's not here. Even if she were, I doubt she'd speak to you. I'm pretty sure she's moved on, you know?"

Now I was just being a dick, but the kid had it coming. My words were like a punch to the stomach, based on his deflating physique and facial expression.

"Run along, Joe. If I see her, I'll tell her you stopped by." While I was talking, I steered him toward the door without laying a hand on him. Whether I talked a good talk or not, the last thing I needed was trouble with the university. This was the exact kind of student to make my life a living hell.

His demeanor turned on a dime, and instantly he was angry again. "It's Joel," he said, nearly shouting. "My name is Joel, and you can't tell me what to do. Or to leave. Or stay. I came here to talk to Maye."

I took a step back. "And I told you she's not here."

"Where is she?" he demanded.

"How the hell should I know? She's my intern, dude. Not my BFF. Leave right now, and we'll forget this happened. Keep shouting at me, and my nosy coworkers will be in here to see what's going on, and then you're going to wish you had left when advised to do so."

"My father will—" he began to threaten just as my door flew open.

It was Ms. Donnio, exactly as I predicted, and she wore a mixture of curiosity and concern on her unattractive face.

"What's going on in here? Andrew, do you want me to call security?"

"That won't be necessary. This young man was just leaving. Weren't you, son?"

"I'm not your son, old man." He muttered the last part under his breath as he pushed past Rebecca, almost knocking her over.

With her usual tendency for overreacting, she threw herself out of his way much more physically than necessary.

I rolled my eyes at the show and ushered her out the door right after the kid.

"Thank you for checking to see what the commotion was. I owe you one." With that, I shut the door and leaned my back against it. What a ridiculous way to end a ridiculous week.

If I considered just that interaction with that young

nutcase, I'd have to question if associating with Maye Farsey was worth the trouble. But the truth was so much more complex. The past two days had been interminable without her here to brighten this shabby office. Even the work—the very same work I'd always been passionate about—didn't hold the same appeal without her across our much-too-small shared desk to enjoy it with.

I'd had so much time in my own head. Analyzing and overanalyzing what it was exactly about that young lady that enthralled me so completely. In total candidness with myself, I labored over listing the traits that lured me to her. And no kidding, I was brutally honest with myself.

What would probably surprise most people who didn't know me very well was that our vast age difference wasn't even on the list. I'd never been one of those men who found young women appealing. Likely because I interacted with students all the time. I was too aware of the immature, insecure, and flighty tendencies my female students possessed. Definitely not the things I looked for in a mate.

But not Maye. I smiled just thinking about how different she was. Not just from her peers but most of the women I'd ever dated. She was thoughtful in a way most people weren't. She existed beyond herself, and it was obvious in so many ways.

One time in class, I'd watched from behind the monitor of my laptop when she didn't know I had my eye on her. She helped a classmate pick up the contents of her handbag while everyone else stepped around them, grumbling and even laughing about the mishap.

Now, to some, that might not seem like a big thing, but that very same girl she'd helped had been vocally critical of Maye just days before. To the extent that Maye had left class early. But the beautiful, graceful, and kind object of my desire set that experience aside and helped, simply because someone needed a hand. She was made of goodness and light, and it was so damn rare.

She was also organized and methodical in the things she did. Two habits I valued in my own life. Seeing a woman her age with the discipline and focus she had captured my attention early on. And then held it for the entire semester, leading me to choose her specifically for this internship. I knew she'd be the perfect person for the position. The incredible spark that we discovered between us was just icing on the cake.

Or a major roadblock, I supposed, depending on who you asked. I was choosing to embrace it, celebrate it, explore every aspect of it. From what I could tell, Maye was on board with doing the same.

Granted, I wasn't always the best at reading women. I'd had enough practice through the years, but females were a confusing species. There was no other way to say it.

I packed my things and locked the office door on my way out. After the drama with the boy, I decided I was too exhausted to go be social. But I promised myself I wouldn't text or call Maye again until the following day. I didn't want to come on too strong, but it was taking every ounce of self-control to not hit her number on my phone's screen.

Thankfully, there was no sign of her ex when I left the building and headed across the lot to my dusty car. There had been some sort of staff enrichment thing at the building the first half of the day, so when I arrived that morning, the lot was much more crowded than it usually was in the summer months.

About halfway to my car, I heard a vehicle enter the lot at the closest driveway to where I walked. When the unremarkable sedan began to accelerate, instinct told me I was in trouble. As the car closed in closer, the whole scene shifted into slow motion. Including my own reactions.

One moment, I saw the driver glaring right at me. The next moment, the hard thud of the pavement meeting my skull shook me to my core.

Darkness closed in as I lay motionless on the ground. The squeal of tires skipping across the street played a strange, unsettling lullaby as I faded into unconsciousness.

CHAPTER TWELVE

MAYE

By Sunday evening, I was alternately heartbroken and livid. The period between the two swapping had ballooned to hours by that point, and I was solidly stuck with my ire. The problem was finding the right target for my fury. Was I angrier with myself or Andrew? It was definitely a toss-up at that point.

I swore I wouldn't get into any sort of relationship with the man with blinders on. And I used that term in its loosest form. We weren't in a relationship. Outside of him being my teacher and I his foolish, starry-eyed student, at least. I felt like a naïve, ignorant, gullible little girl for buying into his routine.

So yeah, that settled it—I was really pissed at myself.

The excuses I made up in my head for him had run their course. The goodwill points he'd earned with the bedside visit had been whittled to nil. I was lying on my bed with tear-swollen eyes when Shepperd rushed into our room.

She had been noticeably absent the past few days, and I was so glad to see her. Even though our relationship was nothing like it used to be, she was still my best friend. I needed someone to talk to about Andrew ghosting me, but she rushed through the door and straight into our shared walk-in closet, stripping her gym clothes as she went.

"Girl, where have you been?" I asked while sitting up

against my headboard. "And where's the fire now?"

She ducked her head out of the closet and said, "Oh, hey. Didn't even see you there when I walked in. Sorry."

"Are you going out? Why the Tasmanian Devil impersonation?"

As she tightened the belt on her robe, she reemerged from the walk-in and stopped short beside my bed when she got a good look at my face.

"You crying? What's going on?" My twin finally halted her whirlwind momentum and plunked down onto my mattress, right beside my hip. "Who do I have to kill?"

"Where have you been most of the week, Shep? Classes are done, and you can only work out so much." My questions weren't intended to sound like an interrogation, but when my sister tensed like she was about to jolt back to her feet and forget any tenderness she was considering, I clutched her wrist. "I've been missing you, that's all."

"Maye, what's going on? I can totally tell you've been crying, so don't try to bullshit me. Please tell me." She paused a few seconds, rolled her eyes heavenward, and exhaled. "Please tell me this isn't over that dumbass, Joel."

I made a poor excuse for a laugh to set her mind at ease. "No, he's so far back in my history book, he would have to reference the index to catch up with my life now."

"Good. Shit, I'm glad that was your answer. Then who has you this upset? The 'rents?"

Because I had interrupted her on her way to the shower, she sat on my bedside in just her robe. As it slid apart while she gesticulated, something we all did when we talked, I was catching glimpses of her bare frame. I could see every rib in her chest, and it was unsettling. I knew the moment I said anything about it, though, she'd bolt from the room. Selfishly, I really needed an ear, so I averted my eyes and admitted what was going on.

"It's Andrew," I said quietly.

"Andrew?" she asked, her face twisted with confusion. "Professor Chaplin?" Immediately her expression changed to a sly grin. "So it's Andrew now, is it?"

"I don't understand what's going on with him. He came here to visit the day I got this cast put on." After lifting my arm as a visual reference to said cast, my gaze naturally went to the dying bouquet of flowers on my dresser. With my uninjured hand, I rubbed the ache that stabbed in the center of my chest.

"Right. So what? Did Mom and Dad scare him off?" Shepperd was first to think the worst of our parents. Just because she didn't get along with them these days, she thought none of us could have an amicable relationship with them either.

"No. Nothing like that. That night when he left, everything was fine. I even spoke with him the day after that. He texted me throughout the following two days and mentioned going out with some colleagues for happy hour on Friday."

"Help a sister out here, Maye. None of what you're telling me is worth crying over. I get that you may feel insecure about him going out with his peers, but really, you can't act that immature, or you'll drive him away," she advised. "Older guys don't want to be bogged down with schoolgirl drama."

In the past, jealousy would've been my go-to reaction with other boyfriends. Often, I'd get possessive and accusatory right out of the gate without hearing their side of the story. I'd battled insecurity most of my life and had always blamed it on being the invisible half of a pair. But I hadn't felt that way with

Andrew at all. Everything he said and did with regard to our burgeoning attraction made me feel confident and beautiful. Seen.

"I swear, Shep, I didn't act like I normally do. He's given me no reason to feel insecure. Even that night, I was genuinely happy he was going out with his work friends. I encouraged him to do it when he was on the fence about joining them."

"Ooohhhkaaay," she drew out across more beats than necessary. But my twin was snarky and impatient right out of the womb. I didn't expect her to coddle me now that I was obviously emotionally fragile. "So what's going on? This isn't really making sense."

"To me either," I explained. "Friday night we said our goodbyes, and he's been ghosting me ever since. And that's not like him at all. Since I've been laid up here"—I lifted my enormous blue cast again—"he's been very attentive. It's been sweet, actually." I couldn't help the smile that spread across my lips when I admitted that. My sister matched my expression and gave my thigh a reassuring pat.

"Then there must be a logical explanation for the whole thing," she said in a tone more upbeat than I'd heard from her in months. I watched her carefully as she rose and tightened her robe.

Biting my tongue about her weight loss, I said instead, "God, Shep, I hope you're right. I just don't know how else to get a hold of him."

"You know where he lives, right? You were there the night you got hurt?"

I nodded, trying to keep up with her possible idea. When I didn't say more, she blurted, "Then go there." She gave me her patented *duh* look. "Knock on his fucking door, and get some answers."

It was my turn with the expression indicating she wasn't using her brain to its fullest capacity. "I can't drive. Not yet, at least. I have to wait until my appointment on Tuesday for the doctor to clear me to get back behind the wheel. And"—I held up my flat hand to stop her rejoinder because she already had sucked in a breath to let one fly—"before you suggest I drive anyway, Mom was right there when the doctor explicitly said not to."

She shook her head and grinned that evil, mischievous grin she had perfected. "You're such a rule follower." She glanced at the clock on her nightstand and shot back to her warp-speed movement around our room. Gathering her things for a shower, she paused by the door on her way down the hall to the bathroom.

"I have an idea," Shepperd said.

"I'm listening."

"I have some downtime tomorrow afternoon. Like around four. I'll drive you over to his place if you don't hear from him by then. Sound good?" She waited for me to approve the plan and then disappeared out the door.

In a few moments, I heard the bathroom door slam and the shower kick on.

About ten minutes later, my mother's tentative knock pulled me from my daydreaming. Since Shep had gone to the shower, I'd been imagining every possible outcome of showing up at Andrew's house uninvited. From finding him in a compromising position with another woman to him dead on the toilet with his pants around his ankles—I had visited every plausible and ridiculous scenario in my imagination.

"Darling? Can I get you anything?" Her gentle smile

warmed my aching heart.

"Hey, Mom. Nah, I'm good here. Plus, it's just a broken arm. I can do things for myself." I sat up taller and announced with confidence, "I'm actually thinking about going out with Shep tomorrow afternoon." At her surprised reaction, I added, "You know, to get some fresh air. Sunshine?" That explanation softened her facial features, so I added for good measure, "I've been going a little stir-crazy just lying around. Never good for my head, you know?" I tapped my temple with my index finger a couple of times, and she gave me a hearty nod.

"I think that's a great idea, honey. And I'm even happier to hear you're going with your sister." Conspiratorially, she whispered, "What has her barreling around here? She's been manic since she walked in the door."

"I'm not really sure. We were talking before she went to shower, but I was selfish and having a pity party for one. I didn't even ask her what she had going on." Great! Now I piled on guilt to the already full self-loathing I was pummeling my psyche with.

"I'll see what I can find out when she comes back in," I offered.

I was the only one Shep really talked to in the house these days, so I was often enlisted to investigate what my twin was up to. Not really a bad thing. I knew their concern was genuine. It was the reporting back that always made me feel like a traitor. Not that I necessarily told them everything I discovered, of course. The loyalty to my twin would always trump any other relationship I had.

"Your father and I just worry about her," Mom explained unnecessarily. "You know that, right?"

"Of course I do. After raising Hannah and Agatha, I'm

sure you've learned there are some things you don't want or need to know regarding your twentysomething daughters, though," I said lightheartedly.

My words had the desired effect, and she went on her way.

Shepperd's frantic behavior continued over the next hour while she dried her hair and put on enough makeup for the both of us.

"Where are you going?" I finally asked after watching her whip the third black outfit off a hanger so forcefully, the empty hanger flipped off the bar and smacked her in the face.

"For fuck's sake!" she shouted, and I snickered. I could plainly see she wasn't injured, so I wasn't being a total jerk by laughing.

I got out of bed and cautiously approached. "Want some help?" I asked quietly.

She gave me a look I'd seen a hundred times. It was her nonverbal stand-in for *be serious*, and regardless of how often she treated me to the expression, it always stung.

"What?" I snapped and was surprised at my own tone. I was tired, and my arm hurt, but she didn't deserve that. "Sorry," I muttered. "But I don't understand why you act like I couldn't possibly be of assistance."

"It's not that, Mayday. I mean, not in general. But with clothing? Yeah, I guess it is. You know our styles are completely opposite. I'm already frustrated with this situation." She waved a fully extended arm in the direction of her side of our closet. "I don't want to also entertain offers for a style makeover."

"Well, that's not what I was going to do. I thought I could help you pick something from your side," I explained meekly.

"Sorry. I didn't know that."

"No, you didn't. Because you're always so short-tempered

and closed off. You don't let anyone help you with anything."
I knew this girl better than anyone. That would be the only
comment I'd get in beyond surface-level pleasantries. She
typically flipped her mood switch after a single comment
regarding her temperament.

"I don't need anyone's help. Nor do I need the guilt trip
that always follows, you know?" she answered while tugging a
formfitting dress over her hips.

Yep, here we go.

"When have I ever guilted you for needing help? That's
just not true, and it's not very fair."

I had no idea what compelled me to keep this conversation
going tonight. Normally I would've shut my mouth and just
left her alone. All the crap going on with Andrew and the damn
incessant painful throbbing in my arm made me curt, however.

"I don't want to argue with you, Maye. You're right. That
was unfair of me to say to you specifically. Sorry. Now if you
don't mind, I'm going to be late."

"Where are you going? I've asked like three times, and
you keep evading the question one way or another. Why won't
you tell me? You look like fire, by the way."

And she did. Her body was way too thin for anything but a
bodycon-style dress. Even that hung more than it was designed
to in certain areas, but I would never add to her already fragile
and distorted body image by saying something about it.

Shepperd exhaled pointedly and said, "I have a date." The
admission was immediately followed by her full-stop hand
gesture before I had a chance to ask anything else.

"I'm begging you not to harass me with a litany of
questions now that I told you." She huffed impatiently.

"I'm just excited for you, Shep. That's not a bad thing."

This perpetual guard she had up was exhausting to constantly butt into.

My sister gave herself one last look in the full-length mirror on the inside of our closet door and apparently was content with what she saw.

"You look fantastic. Someone will be very happy to see you tonight."

"Thanks, Maye. Cover for me with the units if this runs long?" she asked by way of the mirror. Regardless of how bitter her temperament, I'd always have her back, so of course I gave a quick dip of my chin.

"You're the best twin ever," she said and scooped up her purse from where she had tossed it on her bed earlier.

"Do I know the guy you're seeing tonight?" I asked, desperate for her to stay a little longer. Talking with her was the most excitement I'd had all day. The minute she left, I'd sink right back into my own head.

"No, you don't know him. His name is Lawrence, but everyone calls him Law. It's the dude from the gym I was telling you about," she admitted. "But I really have to go. I'll talk to you tomorrow, because I'm sure you'll be sleeping when I get home."

With a grin, I teased, "I may have to wait up for you just to get the scoop about how the date went."

"Don't," she shot back instantly. But then softened the rough edges of her response with, "I have no idea how late I'll be. You need to rest."

And with that last mini glimpse of concern, she was off.

I fell asleep soon after, thanks to the pain medicine finally doing its thing. Fitful dreams tormented me most of the night, however. When morning came, I felt worse than when I went to bed.

My mom helped me wash my hair. It was as good as any comedy routine trying to wash and rinse my long hair in our kitchen sink, but what were the options? There was no way I could do this for six or eight weeks. I'd have to schedule weekly appointments at my regular salon to have it washed and styled, and I felt sick when I thought about the toll that would take on my savings account.

How had everything gone from amazing to complete shit in a matter of days? On top of my personal hygiene dilemma, I still hadn't heard a word from Andrew.

The realization that whatever was brewing between us was probably over before it had started was starting to settle in. I still alternated between sadness and anger when I thought about it for too long, so I did my best to avoid thinking about it. Lame, I know, but I had shifted into survival mode. I couldn't spend another day lying in bed feeling bad for myself. It just wasn't my style.

By the time Shepperd got home, it was almost six p.m. I texted her around four thirty, asking if she was still up for taking me to Andrew's, and she explained she was stuck in traffic and doing her best to get home. She looked like a nest of hornets had taken up residence in the back seat of our shared car by the time she walked in the front door.

"There are days I literally hate this city," she spewed as she dropped face-first onto her bed.

Since I'd been waiting for her for hours, I was fresh-faced and ready to go and suddenly feeling very guilty that she'd have to get back in the car.

"Hey, listen...if you're not up for driving me over to his house, I get it. I know sitting in traffic can suck the life out of you."

It dawned on me that I didn't know what she'd been up to all day. Classes were finished, and the gym she used was close to the house. There would be no need to get on the freeway.

"Where were you all day?" I asked as she sat up.

"Just let me grab a Monster or something to perk up, and I'll be ready to leave," she said instead of answering my question. This routine was getting so familiar.

"Shep?" I paused until she turned back to look at me from the doorway of our room. "Why do you keep doing that? I asked you where you were."

"Yes, Mom. I heard what you asked me," she said impatiently. "Do you want me to drive you or not? Let's go."

Maybe because I'd been spending so much time inside my head, or maybe it was a side effect of the pain medication, or maybe she was just being a bitch and it hurt my feelings. Whatever the cause, tears filled my eyes as I stared at my twin. The growing crevasse between us widening every time she blew me off.

Shepperd rushed toward me, face twisted in frustration. Through gritted teeth, she said in a quiet hiss, "I got a job. Okay? But it's in the fucking Valley, and the drive sucks."

Was that the truth? I had no way to tell these days with her, but why make something like that up? Why avoid telling me in the first place?

"Oh, okay." I sniffled. "Thank you for telling me. I'm sorry I made you mad, Shep. I just don't like this feeling between us all the time. I feel like I'm losing you, and it scares me."

"Don't be so dramatic, Maye. I get that you're lovesick, and everything else is going on"—she motioned to my arm— "but you're not losing me. I'm right here. I'm just dealing with a lot right now." With that admission, she turned and walked out.

I quickly followed because I didn't want her to drive off without me.

Once we were in the car, I gave her directions to Professor Chaplin's house. It wasn't a far drive, and we could avoid the freeway to get there. We barely spoke on the way, and the tension amped up my already frazzled nerves.

Shifting in the passenger seat, I admitted, "I'm so nervous."

"Do you think he's with someone else?" my twin asked, finally looking at me while we sat at a traffic light.

"Maybe. There is this other teacher," I began, thinking of Ms. Donnio. "Her office is next to his, and she's always coming on to him. It's embarrassing and awkward to witness, honestly."

"You think they're hooking up?"

"I didn't before, but if nothing else, these past few days have been a reminder of how little I know about the guy. But shit, Shepperd, I'm not joking, the chemistry we have is so good. I've never been so intrigued by a man."

"I think they get more interesting the older they are. They have more life story behind them, you know?"

"Hmm, maybe. I mean...that makes sense," I said and pointed through the windshield. "That's it up ahead. Where that red car is."

There was a red sedan in Andrew's driveway. It definitely wasn't his car. I knew that for a fact. His car was black and sportier than that thing. My stomach was in knots as my sister pulled into the driveway alongside the other vehicle.

"So what's the plan?" she asked, taking way more delight in our mission than I was.

"I'm not sure. I guess I'll just go ring the bell. My God..." I whimpered that last part. "What if he's rude or mean? What if he's in there with someone?"

She shrugged like it was just another day. "Well, then you know he's a douchebag, and you move on." It really was that simple in her mind.

"I'll feel like such an idiot. Such a child." I cradled my face in my palms, which I'm sure looked ridiculous with the big blue cast.

Why I let my mother talk me into the blue fiberglass, I'd never know. As if the thing wasn't huge and obvious on its own, it was bright blue like a cop car beacon to boot.

"You'll feel better knowing," she encouraged. "I'll wait here with the engine running so we can bolt if we have to."

I swung my gaze her way so fast, my neck audibly cracked. "Wait...what? You're not coming with me?" I thought for sure she'd come to the door with me. I had counted on it, actually.

"No, you go. It'll be better. He won't feel so cornered if he's in there. Go." She urged me out of the car with a wave of her hand. "Get it over with. You're just sitting there getting yourself psyched up about it."

She wasn't wrong. But then again, she knew me better than anyone else ever had or probably ever would. I gave myself a fortifying nod, reminding myself of what the past few days had been like when I thought he was ghosting me.

At the front door, I raised my fist to knock. Then I saw the doorbell and debated which to use to announce my presence. It ended up not being necessary, because while I stood there having an internal argument, the front door swung open. To my surprise, an elderly woman stood in the entrance. She looked as surprised as I was but still managed a kind smile.

"Hello. Can I help you? I thought I heard someone out

here and looked through the peep hole and saw you standing there. Are you lost, dear?" After a second smile was offered, I realized this must be Andrew's mother. The physical resemblance really became obvious when she smiled so warmly.

"Hello. I was hoping to speak to Andrew. Is he home?" I somehow managed to say after choking on the greeting twice.

The woman tilted her head but couldn't hold my gaze. She was struggling with something. I could see her throat constricting as she tried, in vain, I might add, to hold back tears. When she finally did look at me directly, the unmistakable sheen of unexpressed emotion was in her gentle eyes.

Instantly my stomach plummeted all the way to my toes and bounced back like a rubber ball. Something was wrong. I could nearly smell the sadness wafting from the woman. I wanted to step forward and wrap her in my arms more than anything. I just couldn't be sure if it was to comfort her or me in that moment.

My gut was screaming at me that something was terribly wrong and she didn't want to be the one to tell me. Everything about the woman's body language said bad news was coming down and I'd better brace for impact.

So many thoughts flashed through my mind in a millisecond. From possible things that could've happened right down to how did his mother get here from Nebraska? Andrew hadn't mentioned her planning a visit, and the night I spent at his house, we had had a lengthy conversation about his relationship with the woman. Even though there were many miles between them, they remained close. Especially after his father's untimely death.

Finally, she grimaced and asked, "I'm sorry, dear, how do

you know my son?"

I was trembling, and my voice betrayed me when I said, "Did something happen? Is he okay? Where is he?" I had only intended the first question. The second and third leaped from my mouth of their own accord. "I'm sorry," I gushed. "I'm not meaning to be rude."

I quickly realized she wasn't going to tell me anything until I qualified how I fit into her son's life. So I thrust out my hand and offered an introduction.

"I'm so sorry," I insisted again. "My name is Maye Farsey. Dr. Chaplin is my mentor. The professor for my summer internship at the university." *Shit*. Should I not have admitted I was his student? Maybe if I seemed too emotionally invested, now she would get suspicious. Had he mentioned me to his mother in any capacity?

Her hands were frailer than I expected from the rest of her appearance. Her grip was gentle and unsteady, and I met her sad eyes while we shook.

Again, with no thought, I blurted, "Is he here? Is something wrong?"

"Maybe you should come inside, dear." She stood back from where she had been blocking the entrance.

I looked back to the driveway before accepting her invitation.

With a thumb gesture over my shoulder, I explained, "My sister is waiting for me in the car. Let me tell her we are going to be a few minutes, okay?"

"Yes, all right. I'll go put on some tea. Please, invite her in too. I'd hate for her to sit out in the car while we talk." Andrew's mother shuffled off toward the kitchen without waiting for my reply, so I pulled the door closed and hustled back to the driveway to speak to Shepperd.

My twin was busy on her cellphone, so I tapped on the glass, and she jolted.

Sorry, I mouthed while she glared my way and put the window down.

"*Sorry,* I didn't mean to scare you," I said.

But my sister wasn't one to forgive easily. Rather than absolve me from a genuine accident, she forged ahead with her own questions.

"Was he there? What did he say? Where has he been? Why hasn't he called or texted?" She fired the questions so rapidly, I didn't stand a chance of getting a word in to explain.

When I was sure she was done, I grinned. It was a strange reaction given what I was about to tell her, but my expression was in relation to her specifically. When I saw these little glimmers of her nicer, kinder persona leak out through her protective shell's cracks, I held out hope we'd all get our Shepperd back one day. My twin was fiercely loyal and equally protective of the people she loved.

"His mother answered the door." On the fingers peeking out from the end of my cast, I ticked off, "I know for a fact that she lives in Nebraska and that Andrew didn't mention a single word about her coming for a visit. But no, he's not here, and she invited us inside to explain. She didn't want you to sit out here in the car, so pleeeaaase, Shep, come inside with me?"

Whether she was truly considering her actions or just enjoying torturing me, I couldn't tell. Normally I had the girl's number and could read her better than anyone else. But my own nerves were baked, and I couldn't focus on anything but the way my heart thundered beneath my rib cage.

Shepperd let out a dramatic sigh and turned off the engine.

I backed away from the car so she could get out and lock the doors. We walked inside the front door without knocking this time, and I could hear the sound of a kettle whistling from the kitchen.

"In here," I said quietly to my sister and led the way.

Once we stood at the island, I introduced my sister to the elderly woman. Her genuine smile coaxed something similar from Shep, and I was reminded of how beautiful my sibling was. She had always had a soft spot for old people, and it was amazing to see something was still as I knew it within her.

I was desperate for answers. The drawn-out process of pouring tea into cups and fussing about trying to find where her son kept the cream and sugar was about to make me lose my patience. Finally, I had to ask the question burning my heart to smoldering ash.

"Can you please tell me what happened? Where is Andrew?" I asked as kindly as I could manage.

"I got a call a few nights ago." She paused to jog her memory. "Shoot, I don't even know what day it is. They've all blended together since I got here." She sipped her tea, and I noticed the way she trembled. I didn't know much about the woman or her general health, so I assumed she was exhausted.

"Apparently, my son has me as his emergency contact with the university," she continued to recount at a snail's pace. "They were very nice when they phoned."

Oh. My. God. I was losing my mind. I wanted to shake her and shout, *Get to the point!*

Beneath the counter, my sister put a calming hand on my bouncing thigh, and I was reminded to be respectful and compassionate. Clearly, the woman needed to tell the story in her own way. I gave Shepperd a grateful nod, and she withdrew her hand. She'd never know how much that small gesture calmed me.

"You can imagine my panic when they told me he'd been struck by a hit-and-run driver in the school parking lot. Apparently, he had to be airlifted to a nearby hospital, and that's where I've been spending most of my days and nights since I arrived. You're actually very lucky you caught me here tonight. The nurses are so sweet, but they insisted I get some proper sleep and come back in the morning."

"He...he what?" I croaked while clutching my throat. I couldn't breathe.

"Oh, dear, sit down, honey," the woman said. "You don't look so good."

"Is he okay? Do they know who hit him?" Shepperd asked while I tried to pull my shit together.

"Well, it was touch and go at first. Andrew hit his head when he went down—or so they think. He has no memory of the accident happening. At least not yet. But today was the first day he was able to speak after they removed that awful tube." She motioned to her mouth and throat, and I surmised that he had been intubated. "The doctors are hopeful he will make a complete recovery. They just can't say how long that will take." She dabbed tears from the paper-thin skin beneath her eyes as she told us as many details as she could recall.

Through the whole retelling of the facts, I sat motionless. I couldn't even process a fraction of the thoughts running through my head. Who would do such a thing? Yes, Andrew was known to be a tough teacher. It was hard to get an A in any of the classes he taught, and his expectations from his students typically outweighed their performances.

Could a former student harbor that much resentment to

attempt to kill him?

I mean...that had to be what was intended here, right?

Again, my twin saved me from wasting this woman's time by asking the right questions.

"What hospital did you say he's being treated at, Mrs. Chaplin?"

"Please, call me Millie. All my friends have always called me Millie," she said and gave my sister's hand a little squeeze. "I have the address of the place in my purse. I'll give it to you before you leave."

"I'd really appreciate that," I barely whispered.

Shepperd took the last gulp from her pretty porcelain teacup and carried mine and hers to the sink.

"Oh, dear, you don't have to worry about that," Millie insisted. "I'll clean up in a bit when I have some energy."

"It's no bother at all. But I think we've kept you long enough. Haven't we, Maye?" It wasn't until she said my name that I registered she was talking to me.

"Oh, my goodness," Millie said, and covered her grin with her bluish hand. All the blood vessels were so close to the surface, it changed the perception of their hue. "I didn't put two and two together when you first introduced yourself," she said to me with the biggest smile.

With my overly active brain at the moment, I couldn't understand what she was getting at. I tilted my head to the side a bit and waited for her to finish her thought.

"He's been asking for you. Relentlessly." She smiled my way and gave my hand another squeeze. "You must be very special. I'm glad we were able to have a cup of tea together. Chat a bit."

Shepperd tugged my sleeve to pull me out of the trance

I kept dipping in and out of. How could I not be lost at that point? I'd been on the emotional equivalent of a roller coaster since admitting I had feelings for the man. Feelings deeper than I thought I even realized, based on the amount of giddy relief overwhelming me. Tears came unbidden, and I wouldn't be able to hold it together much longer.

"I'm so sorry," I said through a strangled laugh. I swiped my cheeks over and over, but the tears were coming hard then. "You have no idea how worried I was when I didn't hear from him," I gushed through my waterworks.

"Well, I'm so glad you stopped by," Millie said while escorting us to the front door. "Put your mind to rest, dear." She swept me into a long hug, and I greedily accepted the comfort. When we separated, she said, "Thank you for caring for my son. I think you're a bit young," she said, smiling earnestly with her honesty, "but he needs a good woman in his life. He works too much and has become a bit of a homebody." Saying that made her giggle. Then she revealed, "He'd kill me if he knew I said that." She shrugged, "Oh well. Mother's prerogative, right? Maybe I'll see you again before I head home?"

"I'd like that," I said truthfully and stood in amazement as the woman hugged my sister and Shepperd returned the embrace. Normally she stood with her straight arms by her sides until the other person gave up from the embarrassment of an unrequited gesture of affection.

"Get some rest, Millie," my sister called from the front walk. "He's going to need you at your best. Especially when they release him, I'm sure."

Who the hell was the woman getting into the driver's seat of our shared car? I hadn't seen or heard a sign of kindness from my sister in so long, she seemed like a stranger.

Once buckled in, she started the car, and I alternated staring at her and staring out the front windshield. My thoughts were going in so many different directions, it was hard to pluck one from the whirlwind and expand upon it.

"I can't thank you enough for doing that with me. I feel like my head's going to explode, though, with all the information we just learned. Who would do that? They probably have security camera footage, wouldn't you think?"

"Yeah, I would think so," Shepperd agreed as she backed out of the driveway. Once the car was in drive, she continued her train of thought. "But who's in charge of that? Who looks at that footage and determines who's at fault? I'm sure we won't be part of that conversation, no matter who it is."

"Right? But maybe I could help identify the person. You know, if they have trouble?" For the most part, I was thinking out loud. I didn't know who his enemies were. The only person I'd ever seen Andrew get in a confrontation with was Joel.

In a panic, I gripped my twin's arm even though she was driving. The car swerved slightly, but she had a handle on it.

"Maye! What the fuck are you doing? You're going to get us killed."

"Sorry," I rushed out. "I just thought of something— something bad."

"Ohhhkaaay. Great. That doesn't mean we need to get in an accident over it."

"You're right, you're right. I'm sorry. I wasn't thinking." I copped to my mistake and explained my concern. "What if it was Joel?"

My sister looked at me like I sprouted a second head. "Your ex, Joel? Why would he have anything to do with this?"

"Remember I told you what happened the night I fell?

When he got physical with me?"

"Yeah, but that's no reason to try to kill someone."

"I agree. But he wasn't acting rationally that day. I saw a different, frightening side of him that I had never seen before."

We were quiet in our own thoughts for a few miles before Shepperd asked, "So what are you gonna do now? Go to the hospital, I'm assuming?"

"Absolutely. But I probably have to wait until tomorrow. That visit took longer than I thought it would, and I doubt visitors are welcome at this hour at the hospital."

"Good point. Although"—she gave me a mischievous grin—"why let that stop you?"

"Because I'm the good girl, remember? The rule follower." I sighed and slumped back in the seat. "Before you say anything, yes, I hear how lame that sounds. You think I always want to be exactly what everyone thinks I am?"

"Give me a break, Maye," she said with zero sympathy or compassion.

I looked at her without hiding my frustration, and she went on. "You're the only one with the power to be who you want to be. You can't play the victim to the lottery of life all the time. If you don't like the perception everyone has of you, change it."

"That's so easy for you to say," I muttered while looking out my side window.

"No, it's just the truth. No one wants to hear the truth or, God forbid, speak it. That house we live in? Everyone walks around pretending to be the perfect little all-American family when the reality would horrify people. We have more dysfunction than the Spellings."

"The Spellings?" I laughed the question. "So random,

Shep. Seriously..."

She laughed her throaty laugh, and the tension was instantly sliced. I didn't want to argue with my sister tonight. I was emotionally exhausted, and her issues with our family were so deep and complicated, I suspected it was going to take a professional to sift through them with her.

I just hoped she took on the challenge before it was too late.

CHAPTER THIRTEEN

ANDREW

"Now push against my hand," the doctor instructed as we went through the daily exam. It had been a week since someone struck me down like the last standing pin in the tenth frame. The police were diligently—according to them—investigating the accident, and I would ensure the responsible party was punished to the fullest extent of the law.

I had a good idea who was behind the wheel of the car that night in my office building's parking lot based on the exchange I had with that kid obsessed with Maye. But so much about the incident was unclear, and on the slim chance it wasn't him, I didn't want to bring attention to what was going on between Maye and me.

The whole thing was a fucking mess, and to top it all off, I hadn't been able to see her once. We spoke briefly on the phone a couple of days ago, but I was climbing the walls of the orthopedic rehabilitation center I was moved to last night. I didn't need to be here. In my opinion, at least. The medical team caring for me was exercising an abundance of caution, the head doctor explained, because of the delicate nature of the accident.

Delicate? What's so delicate about a one-and-a-half-ton Toyota mowing me down?

My mother sat quietly in the corner of my room. The night nurse brought her a blue vinyl monstrosity of a piece of furniture, but at least she wasn't left to stand or perch at the foot of my bed like before that eyesore arrived.

I blamed the miserable combination of pain, lack of sleep, and concern for Maye for my disagreeable temperament. My mother, who by all accounts was a saint among the living, even gave up cheering me up and sat across the room silently working on a sewing project.

As long as I could remember, she had always done needlepoint when things weren't going well. She said it calmed her nerves and occupied her mind so she didn't fixate on the negative.

When the doctor finished his exam, he added a few notes to my chart, gave some praise about my progress, and promised to be back before the end of his shift to check on me.

Awesome.

"Doctor?" I said just before he was out the door.

"Hmm?" he asked. Already with phone in hand, he finished typing before looking up and giving me his full attention.

"Any idea how long I'll be here? I have a job I'm worried about, and—"

The young doctor came back to stand beside my bed. He was kind and smart and had a great sense of humor when I was in the mood for it.

"I know it can be maddening lying in bed all day, staring at the same four walls or the dummy box. I'll let your nurse know she can start taking you out for short walks, maybe to the healing garden on the ground floor. That will break up the monotony a bit. Plus, the fresh air and sunshine can do wonders for your spirit."

"Okay, that's great. I guess?" I had no idea what a healing garden entailed and couldn't fathom how I'd go out on a walk—short or long—in my current condition other than being pushed around in a wheelchair. "But if I'm going to lie around most of the day, couldn't I do that at home? I could have a home health nurse come visit at my place."

I knew statistics showed that patients healed quicker in their own environments. I wasn't trying to tell the guy how to do his job, but I wasn't above it if it meant I could get the hell out of this depressing place.

"I like the way you're thinking, man!" he said in a tone much too bright for the conversation. "Can I shoot straight with you right now?" He sat on the edge of my bed, keeping a respectful distance but creating a more intimate conversation.

"Yeah, go for it. I'd appreciate it, actually."

"You've got some work ahead of you. I know this place isn't the Ritz. I know you probably have a sweet wife or girlfriend holding things down at home, coming unglued from the stress and worry. Right now, you need to put all your energy into staying positive and getting well. You have to put you at the top of the list for a change and do what needs to be done here." He stabbed his index finger into my mattress. "So you can get back to being the kick-ass guy you were before this accident. But we have to take certain steps in a certain order. But you control the pace. No one else can put in the hard work for you."

While I appreciated the pep talk, I certainly didn't feel better. Plus, I didn't miss the way he avoided answering my actual question. But instead of treating the guy like my shrink, I forced a smile and quietly thanked him.

"I know you're busy," I choked out. "I appreciate you coming back and saying all of that."

"I guarantee we don't want you in here any longer than you need to be. But I wouldn't be doing my best as your doctor if I sent you home before you were ready. You have to trust that, okay?" He gave the mattress a rapid double pat and stood.

"Thanks, Doc," I said and let the guy get back to work.

My mother cautiously approached the bed, and I felt like the biggest ass. I knew my mood was shit, but she actually looked nervous to approach me. I hadn't raised my voice. Hell, I hadn't even voiced any of that to her before I had to the doctor.

"Mom," I sighed. "What's wrong?"

"Oh, Andrew," she warbled. "No matter how old you are, it's so hard for me to see my child in pain. I know you don't understand that and probably won't until you have children of your own." She clutched the dainty cross on the gold chain around her neck like she always did when wishing for grandchildren. "God willing, someday," she muttered to the ceiling. "If I could do something to make this better, I would."

"Are you sure you've told me everything Maye said when she came to the house? I don't understand why she hasn't come by," I blurted and heard how petulant and whiny I sounded. *Fuck it.* Not seeing her was probably the biggest reason for my foul mood, and I kept tap-dancing around it like it wasn't true.

"Yes, of course I told you everything. I'm not senile yet, young man." She pushed my thigh playfully, not that I could feel it. But before I could go down that path of pity again, she added, "I know I'm just a silly old woman, but why don't you call her? Ask her to come see you?" My mother's sweet face was drawn and tired as she waited for an answer.

An answer I didn't have.

"You're not silly," I said in a lighter tone, hoping to move on from this topic now that my mom positioned herself to give me advice about my love life.

"Very clever, Andrew. Maybe you're feeling better after all, hmmm? Well enough to tease your mother anyway?"

We were quiet as my mom fidgeted with the blankets covering my lower half. "Maybe it's hard for her because of the arm?"

The comment seemed random because of the time that had passed between it and the last mention of Maye.

"What do you mean?"

"Well, I told you her twin sister was with her, right? She had to drive since your friend's arm is in that enormous cast." My mother reflected for a moment with a genuine smile. "My goodness, what a lovely pair of young ladies. Their parents should be very proud."

I wasn't sure if the pain medication was finally starting to work or if this was one of my mom's classic disjointed conversations. Normally, I was much more adept at keeping up with her topic hopping, though.

"I'm not following," I admitted while blinking heavy eyelids.

"I think it's time for a little nap, dear. You just heard what the doctor said about making your own health the priority. Maybe taking his advice would be a good idea?"

Even though she asked it like a question, I knew the woman well enough to know she was really making her opinion known with the remark. She wasn't nearly as clever as she thought. The tactic worked better when I was a boy and a lot more naïve.

"Trust me, Mom. No one wants to be up and out of this bed more than me," I said to appease her and, for whatever it was worth, to start planting seeds of positivity in my own mind. I knew that doctor made good points, even if he looked young enough to be one of my students.

Currently, I couldn't feel anything below my hips. On either side. The fucker hit me at the perfect spot and caused trauma to my spinal cord. My doctor, despite being a baby, was well known throughout the orthopedic community. He expected me to regain sensations gradually as the swelling around my spinal cord decreased.

In the meantime, a torturous physical therapist named Mara worked with me twice a day to maintain my muscle tone and range of motion. The woman was a ballbuster, and even though she was no bigger in stature than Maye, she was strong and tenacious. Every time I complained or gave up on an exercise, she'd bark at me about not quitting and urge me to stay the course. I hated those damn sessions every day. Two times each day I got an hour-long reminder about how weak and pathetic and dependent I was.

Dependent.

Even thinking that word made me want to pull the covers over my head, settle in for a good sleep—and never wake up. If the cops didn't catch that little bastard and throw him in jail, I swore I'd handle things myself.

As soon as I could piss on my own, of course. My mother's shuffling beside my bed made me snap out of my brood. When I looked her way, she had her things packed in the two gigantic tote bags she'd been lugging through the door every morning, and she leaned down to peck my cheek.

"Rest, Andrew. I'll see you in the morning."

"Mom..." I started to tell her she didn't have to come sit here every day but stopped short. The truth was I wanted her to come visit me. If I had to endure this bullshit all alone, I'd surely lose my mind.

"What is it?" she asked when I didn't say more.

"I love you. And thank you—for everything," I choked out through a wad of emotion jammed in my throat, making it difficult to breathe, let alone speak. Unshed tears clouded my vision, so I let my lids close slowly and rest there.

"Oh, honey," she said in the sweetest mom voice of all time. It made the misery in my heart ache even more. "We're going to get through this, I know it. Please keep the faith, okay?" She stroked my greasy hair off my forehead, reminding me I needed a shower but couldn't do that for myself either.

My day nurse, Carrie, said it would be easier for the night nurse to help me with a shower since he was much stronger than she was. At the time, I had no interest in getting out of bed, but now a hot shower sounded like a luxury I'd do anything to enjoy.

"Carrie said Marlin could help me shower tonight. I'll be better tomorrow when you see me," I promised, as if she was judging me for my appearance.

"Don't overdo it. Mara was pretty tough on you today. Maybe save the shower for tomorrow. But of course, that's up to you." She hiked the one tote higher on her shoulder and said, "Okay, dear, I'll see you tomorrow." She gave me another quick kiss, and I watched until the door quietly nestled into its frame.

Like before, when I closed my eyes to get some sleep, my mind started its usual race. I gave up after only a few minutes, knowing how this routine ended every other time. Beneath the covers, I fingered the cellphone beside my thigh and gave in to the temptation.

Her number was first on the recently dialed list. Even

though we hadn't spoken in a couple of days, it wasn't for the lack of trying on my part. I promised myself as the call connected that if I went to her voicemail, I'd preserve whatever was left of my dignity and not leave another plaintive message to call or visit. A man could only grovel so much.

"Hello?" she said so quietly I quickly checked the volume setting on the phone.

"Hey. It— It's Andrew." As if she didn't know that from the caller ID. Idiot.

"Hi. How are you feeling?" she whispered and quickly added, "Give me a minute to go outside."

Interesting. Where was she that she had to go outside? I waited through some shuffling and strained to make out any background sounds I could hear that might clue me in to her location.

Finally, she said in a normal conversational volume, "There. That's better."

I paused for a moment too long, and she said, "Are you still there? Oh no, did I drop you?"

"No, baby, I'm here." I sighed with more contentment than I'd felt in days. "I'm just soaking in the sound of your voice. I miss seeing you so much, Maye."

"Awww, I miss you too," she replied. But then excitedly proceeded to say, "I have exciting news! I'm an auntie!"

"Well, congratulations, that's great." I barely got the response out before she rushed to tell me all the details.

"My oldest sister, Hannah, had her very first baby early this morning. It's a girl, and my God, Andrew, she's the most beautiful little angel you've ever seen. I'll send you a pic if you want to see?"

"Of course I do." My God, I loved hearing her so happy

and full of life. My own mood was immediately improved just from basking in her joy. My phone vibrated, and I pulled it back from my ear to sneak a quick peek at the photo.

"She's beautiful, baby. I trust everyone is well?" I had no experience with births, but I was pretty confident that was the right thing to ask.

"Yes! My sister was amazing, and her husband too. He was so supportive and encouraging. That's the first time I've seen a baby enter the world, and it was fantastic and horrifying all at the same time," she said, giggling.

Well, that explained where she had been the past couple of days when I couldn't reach her. Now I felt like a selfish cad leaving so many messages.

"Sorry I bombed your voicemail. Just delete them all and never mind me."

"I know," she said regretfully. "I'm sorry I haven't been picking up. There were so many times we thought it was the big moment, you know? Then my little niece changed her mind, and the whole process would start again. My poor sister is exhausted. That's why I was so quiet when I answered. She's finally sleeping with sweet Elanor on her chest, and I didn't want to wake them. I think I'll be heading home soon."

"Oh, so you're still at the hospital?" I asked, barely able to get a word in in the midst of her excited rambling.

"No, as crazy as it sounds, they had her at home. But they live in Malibu, so I have a bit of a drive to Brentwood. Tell me how you're doing. I'd be happy to chat while I drive if you're up for it?"

"I'd give my right arm to keep you on the line right now," I said and winced. Maybe that was coming on too strong. The last thing I wanted to do was scare her off by being too clingy or needy. "At least traffic should have died down by now."

"I hope so. I'm so tired from all the excitement. How are you feeling? I bet you're climbing the walls in there."

"They moved me to an orthopedic rehabilitation center yesterday. I have a private room, and my mother spent yesterday and the better part of today here with me while I get used to the new routine."

I can't believe this is my life right now.

"Why did they do that instead of send you home?" she asked innocently, and the part of this conversation I was dreading was already front and center.

But I didn't want to put a damper on her joy. I never wanted to do that for any reason of my own. So instead of answering her question, I clumsily shifted the topic back to the new baby.

"That's a beautiful name they picked. Is it a family name? It's so old-fashioned," I said with as much brightness in my tone that I could manufacture.

"Isn't it? It was Elijah's mother's name. She passed when he was a teenager, and they named the baby Elanor in her honor. The baby looks exactly like my youngest sister, Clemson, when she was a newborn. I have no idea how that happened, but everyone agrees."

Quiet swelled between us when she finished with that explanation.

Finally she said, "Andrew? Why didn't you answer me? Why were you moved to a rehab facility? Will you please tell me what's going on?" Worry was evident in her voice, and I instantly felt like a jerk. No matter which way I tried to handle my shitty news, it was causing her stress.

So I decided to be honest but positive. "My doctors want

me to be under close care for a few weeks while I regain my strength and mobility."

There. Was it sugar-coated? Absolutely. But it was honest and direct, so I had to get some credit for those things, at least. Personally, coming to grips with my situation had been hard enough. Frankly, I still wasn't fully there. It seemed inconceivable to one minute be walking, driving, working—all the things—and the next, well, to be here. Unable to move from the hip down and having no guarantee that I ever would again.

Vomit surged up my esophagus, and I covered my mouth with a loud groan. I dropped the phone into my lap and frantically looked from side to side for something to barf into. The gravity of my physical situation caused a second, more violent lurch from my stomach as I grabbed for the Styrofoam cup on the bed table positioned over my thighs.

Ripping the lid and bendy straw off the top, I tipped my face over the wide brim and revisited the red Jell-O I had for an after-dinner snack. Thank God there wasn't much more in my stomach, because the cup could only hold so much. All the while, Maye was hearing the demoralizing episode from her end of our call, and my hands were too preoccupied to mute the call.

Without thinking beyond the panic and humiliation of what had just happened, I stabbed the button to end the call. Not a word of goodbye nor a mention of talking again soon.

As much as it hurt my heart to conclude, I knew I couldn't let her hang on to hope of any sort of relationship now.

We were already facing tons of backlash because of our age difference and teacher-student relationship. Now, with the added burden of my physical condition, it was all too much. I had nothing to offer the woman but problems, and she deserved so much more than that. The better part of my soul, the unselfish part, knew the best thing I could do for Maye was leave her alone.

I just wasn't sure the other parts of me could do that.

My phone vibrated for the second time as Maye tried to reconnect. I stared at the device and let it ring through to voicemail as my regular night nurse poked his head in the doorway to my room.

"There he is!" he called cheerfully, and I couldn't help but grin. The man's energy was infectious. If ever a person chose the perfect profession, it was this guy.

"Hey, Marlin. How you doing?"

"Can't complain. Carrie said you're needing a shower? Let me get my new admit settled next door, and we'll get you spiffy, 'kay?"

"Not like I'm going anywhere. Whenever you have time. Can you take this, though? Sorry. I think the meds hit my stomach wrong, and there was nothing else nearby," I explained while motioning to the cup.

My nurse bustled into the room. "Oh, that's a bummer. How're you feeling now? Want me to get something ordered for the nausea? In fact, let me check your standing orders. There may be something already written."

"No, don't worry about it. I'm fine now."

"Okay, let me know if you change your mind. No sense feeling worse than you have to, right?" he asked conversationally. Since he was already halfway out the door, though, now with vomit cup in hand, I knew I was keeping him from other patients.

I gave him a quick wave, and he left, the door closing with a quiet *swish*. The vibration of an incoming call was the only sound in my room. I looked down to see Maye's beautiful face on my screen.

I was too lonely and too weak to ignore another attempt. I swiped to answer the call and put the sound on speaker so I could lay more comfortably. *Ha.* That was an oxymoron on this institutional-grade mattress, but I had to keep reminding myself things could be worse.

"Hey there," I said softly.

"Hi. Sorry I dropped the call. Damn canyon gets me every time," she said with her husky laugh. "My God, I haven't been this tired since studying for midterms. I'm going to collapse the moment I get in my room."

"You shouldn't drive when you're that tired. You're not as alert as you should be."

"I'm sure you're right, but everyone else is staying at my sister's, and I have a big day tomorrow."

"Oh? What do you have planned?"

There was an uncomfortable pause, and dread instantly percolated in my gut. If she planned on visiting me, I'd have to come up with a plausible reason why it wouldn't work out. No way in hell did I want her to see me like this. I missed her so fucking bad and knew seeing her would lift my spirits, but at the same time, I planned to try to keep her away until I was further along in my recovery.

"Ummm," she finally said, "I have an internship I committed to?" Her tone was partially teasing but also confused. When I didn't respond, she asked, "I mean, would you mind if I worked in your office while you're not there? I'm sure I could do research from home, but honestly, I get so distracted when I try to work in that house. It's too hectic."

"I haven't personally talked to the dean about the accident

yet," I started to explain.

In her typical optimistic style, she cut me off and said, "I'm sure they'll understand you're going to need some time off. And they shouldn't give you any guff about it either. I mean, the accident did happen on their property."

"The detective working the case said the school has been very cooperative. They definitely don't want it getting out in the media though."

"Oohhkaaay. So what do you have to talk to Dean McCallister about? I don't understand..."

There was no easy way to explain this to her. No matter how I worded it, it was going to be a disappointment. "Listen, Maye, about the internship," I began and came up empty.

I didn't want to admit our time together was over. The concern that everything between us would also end was very real. We barely had a chance to get to know each other. At the time, I didn't stress about it because I figured we could take our time. Let things blossom over the rest of the summer.

"What about it?" she asked shakily. I could already hear the anxiety affecting her voice. The girl was intuitive, no doubt about it.

"Well, baby, I'm not sure how long they're going to keep me here. Then, when I do go home, how long it'll be before I'm in a position where I can go back to work. I'm afraid we'll miss all the submission deadlines by that point. We've already lost another week between your arm and now...this."

"Andrew?"

"Yes, beautiful?"

"I know this is based on my own insecurities, but I feel like there's something you're not telling me." Her confession stabbed me right in the heart. By the way it felt when I inhaled, the same dagger might have grazed a lung, too.

There was no point lying to her. I knew that. But I hadn't come to grips with the truth myself. How could I expect her to take the news in stride?

The first attempt at a response choked me. I was going to lose the girl before I ever had the girl, and I hated it. Hated every damn thing about the situation we were in.

"Why would you feel that way? I've never lied to you about anything. I realize we don't have many chapters in our book together, but you have to know I'm a man of integrity," I said, trying to comfort her.

Silence filled the line for too long.

"I do. I know, I'm sorry. Like I said, it's probably mostly my own insecurities. But something doesn't feel right, and I can't understand why you'd feel like you can't be straight with me."

"Please don't put words in my mouth. Or feelings upon my chest," I replied before thinking too much about it. I winced, though, when the words settled between us. The last thing I wanted was a fight. So I continued to explain, "It's not fair to have to defend something I'm not even feeling or doing, you know?" I asked, trying to appeal to reason while keeping my tone in check.

"No," she said mournfully. "No, it's not fair at all, and I'm sorry. You don't need all my silly manufactured drama while you're trying to recover." Again, the phone line was quiet for a moment. I was choosing the words of my response as carefully as possible when she admitted, "I really miss seeing you."

"God, I miss seeing you too. Shit." I chuckled. "I'd pay money to have you in my arms right now."

"Can I visit you there? Is the rehab place near your home? Or school? Maybe I could come there, and we could work on the submissions from there?" she suggested with cautious hope lacing every word.

"What about driving? My mom said your sister brought you to the house the other day. And you made an incredible impression on her, by the way. I think she's almost as smitten with you as I am." I chuckled through a wide grin.

"Smitten, huh?" she teased. "That sounds about right from where I'm sitting, too."

"Well, I can think of a few other adjectives and adverbs to use when describing my feelings for you. Trust me, I've had a lot of time to think while lying here."

"It's settled, then," she said with finality. "I'll come tomorrow. You can tell me all about these feelings of yours." Her tone was playful but grew serious when she added, "We can get some work done too. If you're up to it, of course."

But I still worried. "If I talk to the dean, and he pulls the plug on the internship program for the summer..."

"Then I'll be very disappointed because I really need that scholarship to help with grad school. But Andrew, internship or not, my feelings for you aren't going to change."

I wanted to reciprocate with the commitment. I wanted it more than anything. But if I didn't regain the use of my legs, I'd never saddle the young, vibrant, intoxicating woman with that. I wanted her to be my girlfriend, not my caregiver. But how the hell did I explain all that to her?

"I'm going to let you go. I'm so tired from the past couple of days, and I want to be fresh and ready to work when I get there tomorrow. Sleep well. I hope you dream of me," she said in the sultriest voice I'd ever heard from her.

And she disconnected the call without another word from me. A war was taking place inside me. My head kept saying don't let her come, but every other part of me was pulling out the poster board and paints to make welcome signs for the woman.

I wanted to hold her in my arms and run my nose along her skin. Just thinking of that morning glory scent and her silky-smooth skin made my dick perk up for the first time since I woke up from the accident.

Thank God for screwed-up miracles. I had deep concern that I had lost sensation between my legs as well, because there hadn't even been the usual morning erection since I'd been hit. But I hadn't allowed myself to think of her in any other way besides not wanting her to see me. Now that I had, I was so damn thankful things seemed to be in working order.

I tossed the phone on the mattress, not really caring where it landed. Now that I'd spoken to Maye, I wasn't interested in much else. Sinking down deeper into the pillows my mom had piled behind me, I really tried to organize my thoughts.

Maye and I barely knew each other on a personal level. We both marveled at the apparent chemistry we shared, but there was so much more to the woman than my physical attraction to her. As if to prove it wasn't a fluke, my cock twitched again as I thought of her.

Marlin would be back for my shower any moment, though. The last thing I wanted to encourage was an erection.

CHAPTER FOURTEEN

MAYE

The moment Shepperd came home, I secured the car for the next day. As soon as the doctor cleared me to drive, I was heading over to see my guy. It was probably silly to think of him as mine, but it made me smile anyway.

Something was definitely off with him when we spoke on the phone, but I chalked it up to the situation he was in. Lying around injured was depressing. No matter how mentally sound you were or how many visitors you had, it was tough dealing with physical limitations.

"I need the car tomorrow," I told my twin. "I have a doctor's appointment."

"I can drop you off," she said as though the car was just hers and she determined the schedule of its use.

"No, that won't work tomorrow. I have things I need to do after the appointment. I can drop you somewhere, though."

"Hell if I'm going to sit around here all day while you run around. Where else do you have to go? I'll either tag along or plan my day around what you need to do."

"Shep, no. I really need the car tomorrow." Maybe changing the subject would be best. I could see all her tells of losing her temper appear, and I was way too exhausted to deal with her. If we started arguing, I'd end up giving in simply because I didn't have the energy to fight.

"Hannah had the baby. Did you get everyone's messages? She was really bummed you weren't there."

"I doubt that," she said with no emotion.

"Shep! Why would you say that?" I asked but mentally checked myself.

She was definitely in a mood, and normally when she was like that, she took every comment and every question as a personal dig.

She flopped on her bed and dug her phone out of her back pocket. "We're not exactly BFFs, you know? I'm sure with everyone else buzzing around, I wasn't even missed."

"So not true." I stared at her for a few moments, but she scrolled on her phone continuously and wouldn't look up.

"Well, she's beautiful and so sweet. Come look at the pictures I took."

She stood and gathered her things for a shower. "Maybe later," she said when she finally met my disbelieving stare. "I need a shower while no one else is in there." She went into our closet for her robe, and when she came out, she asked, "What time is your appointment in the morning? So I'm ready."

"First thing. Eight, I'm pretty sure."

"Ugh, are you serious?"

"When I made the appointment, I was obligated to be at school, so I was trying to miss as little as possible."

"I'll make it work. Anything is better than being trapped here all day," she sneered. "See you in the morning." And with that last comment, she left the room.

I was too tired to deal with her and her moods, so I kicked the whole conversation to the mental curb and drove off. Already nestled in my bed, I sank down deeper beneath the covers and fell asleep immediately.

It was an unusually dreamless night, and before I knew it, the alarm was waking me the next morning. My entire body was stiff from not moving for so long, but I felt incredibly well rested and hopped out of bed and went to find my mom. I wanted to wash my hair and wear it down, knowing I'd be seeing Andrew after my appointment. With the cast on my arm, it was so much easier when someone helped, and who better for the job than my mama?

In the kitchen, she was saying goodbye to someone on the phone, so I waited until she ended her call.

"Was that Hannah?" I asked and grabbed a mug for some coffee. "How is the baby?"

Her smile answered my question, but she added, "They're all doing good. Long night while baby Elanor figures out a routine. The first few weeks are always that way."

I smiled and asked, "Can you wash my hair this morning? I have a doctor's appointment for this thing." I hoisted the cast higher as visual aide "And then I have to meet up with Andrew and work on the grant proposals."

"I thought you said he was in some sort of accident?" she asked. Honestly, I was surprised she absorbed that bit of information. Yesterday, while we were all at Hannah's, I told my sisters about what was going on with Andrew. How we'd had that one night of fooling around, and then of course about what happened with the accident.

My mom was in and out of the room so many times, I thought she wasn't paying attention to what we were talking about. Just more proof—mothers really do hear everything.

"He was. I spoke to him last night on my drive home, and he didn't sound too good." I told her the story while we got everything ready to wash my hair at the kitchen sink. I'd be so glad when this damn cast was off. If I hadn't been so busy the past few days, I would've gone to a salon again to have it washed and blown out. I did that once last week, and it was glorious. Not only having my hair done that day, but not having to deal with it for a total of three days. But, here we were, my head hanging over the stainless-steel farm sink and my mom doing her best to work the shampoo through the mass of long hair.

When we were finished, she asked, "Do you want me to comb it out for you? It's pretty tangled from washing it that way."

"No, I can do it. I know you probably have a Pilates class to get to. I appreciate the help, though. I couldn't imagine how I would've handled that myself."

"Isn't your sister still here? It's awfully early for her to be up and out the door already." Whenever someone said *your sister* to me in a particular way, I knew they were talking about my twin, not one of the others.

"She's still here. I didn't want to wake her, though. You know how she can be first thing in the morning," I explained with an eye roll.

Nodding, my mom said, "Yeah, I sure do. Makes perfect sense. Well, good luck at the doctor's appointment. Let me know how it goes, okay? I better get moving myself." And then she gave me a quick kiss on my cheek before bustling off to her room.

Just as I walked back into my room, Shepperd's alarm was sounding. She pulled the covers down from over her head—the girl slept that way every night—and squinted at her phone. She searched the room until she found me standing by my dresser, watching her.

"Fuck that," she grumbled and burrowed back beneath the covers.

"I'm leaving in twenty minutes, Shep. No ifs, ands, or buts about it. I can't be late for the doctor. They'll make me reschedule."

"Just go without me. Need more sleep."

"No worries. Have a great day when you do get up. I'll be quiet so you can sleep."

Of course, she didn't respond to anything I said, so I grabbed my makeup bag and went to the bathroom to finish getting ready. Honestly, I was glad she wasn't tagging along. I hated having to share a car with her and didn't want to have to worry about where she was and what she wanted to do all day. I just wanted to spend the day with Andrew and not think about anything else.

The doctor cleared me to drive, and it was a good thing since I drove there myself that morning. The pain was nearly gone, and now the cast was just a nuisance. He said I probably had another four weeks to go before I could get it removed, so I made up my mind to deal with it with a better attitude.

Again that morning, Andrew seemed reluctant to give me the name and address of the place he was at. Now that I'd had some sleep, I knew I wasn't misreading his demeanor about the topic, either. It made sense that people didn't like attention or visitors when in a compromised state, but he also said he missed me and was anxious to see me. Mixed signals or not, I made up my mind to stay upbeat and cheerful while I was there, and if it came up again, we could talk about it face-to-face.

I found the place easily, signed in at the front desk as

visitors were required to do, and walked through the long hallway on quiet feet. It was late morning by the time I arrived, so I'd picked up some lunch for us at a sandwich shop nearby.

The place was lovely inside and out. Modern decor and super clean and quiet. So quiet it was unnerving. I paused in front of his door and took a calming breath. I couldn't pinpoint why I was so nervous to see him, but my heart was beating double time.

After a soft knock, I heard his deep voice bidding me to enter.

He was lying in a typical hospital bed, the head raised about two-thirds of the way. He turned and saw me standing in the doorway and sat up a bit straighter. His smile was slow to come but was smart and sexy when it did. Fighting the urge to bound across the room and fling myself onto him, I approached cautiously.

"Hi," I said through a smile. It was so good to see him after worrying so much. "How are you?"

"Maye—" he said, but the last part caught in his throat. Tears filled both our eyes, as I waited for him to say more.

"It's so good to see you. Please— Come to me." He held his hand out toward me, and I grasped it without a second thought.

I stepped close to his bedside while clinging to his palm. His skin felt dryer than it normally did, and the fluorescent lighting above did nothing for the dark circles under his eyes. Bruising marred his handsome face in several spots, and there was a clean bandage, about three inches long, off-center on his forehead.

Seeing him hurt my heart in ways I hadn't expected. I choked back a whimper when he squeezed my hand, bringing my attention back to the present. Tubing from an IV was taped on top where the needle entered his skin.

I bent lower to embrace him, but the position was terribly awkward. "I'm tempted to ask you to shove over so I can climb in beside you," I said on a strangled chuckle. "I want to feel your arms around me more than anything."

"I want that too," Andrew whispered into my hair. "You smell divine, baby. I've missed you more than you know."

"I don't like this," I admitted and felt selfish for doing so at once. There were so many things I wanted to say, and that's what came out? "I meant, I didn't like going all those days without seeing you. I'm becoming attached so quickly." I couldn't read the expression on his face after saying that, and I feared I might have sounded clingy.

He looked like he was in pain. Not necessarily physical pain but tormented. Maybe last night, after he'd tried to come up with every excuse so I wouldn't visit, he came to a different conclusion from our time apart.

Cautiously, I asked, "Does that freak you out? The look on your face right now..."

"No, it doesn't freak me out. I've been going mad without having you near. I'm not sure how this happened so fast either, but I feel the exact same. My own feelings are what scare me."

"You're scared to care about me? Why?" As I gently asked the questions, I made myself comfortable on the edge of the mattress.

He thumbed over his shoulder and offered, "There's a blue chair in the corner behind me. Would you rather sit there?"

I shook my head. "No, I want to sit right here if it's okay with you. I don't want you to be uncomfortable. If I sit back there, I won't be able to see your face while we chat." I cradled his cheek in my palm and gazed down at him.

He leaned into my touch for the briefest second, then pulled back. Maybe all the talk about feelings the moment I walked in the door was too much.

So I straightened and added, "I brought my laptop in case you were up for a little grant work."

Excited, I sprang back to my feet and grabbed the bag I brought in. I was so taken aback when I saw him lying there when I first walked in, I completely forgot I brought lunch.

I plopped the bag on the table that rested over his legs. "I brought us lunch. It's just sandwiches, but my guess is it's better than hospital food. How long did you say you'll have to be in here?" I took a good look around the room for the first time and was hit by a wave of sadness.

The room was small, as most hospital rooms were. When he said he was in a rehabilitation facility, I pictured something a bit more accommodating. More like home.

"I thought these places were a transition between hospital and home?" I asked. "This looks a lot more like a hospital room than a bedroom."

Maybe I was rambling out of nervousness. Andrew hadn't interjected once, and when I turned back to face him, I expected the warm smile he usually had for me. Especially after my nerves had gotten the better of me, and I blathered on about nonsense. Instead, I was met by the serious, almost stern, expression that sucked me back in time to when I was his student.

"What?" I squeaked. "What's wrong?"

"Nothing," he said, but he couldn't hold eye contact for even that one word.

Abandoning the food for now, I went back to perch on the side of his bed. "Do you want to eat at the table? Might feel good to get up and move around a little bit. I'm sure you're stiff from the accident." Having way too much nervous energy pinging around in my body, I shot up again and crossed the room to grab the plastic wand that opened the vertical blinds. Behind them, I found a sliding-glass door that led out to a small balcony.

"Ooooh, this is quaint," I nearly squealed. "We could sit out here? Feel the sunshine?"

"Maye," he said in a tone filled with desperation. Definitely a sound I'd never heard from him before. It had the desired effect, though, because I immediately stopped shuffling around the room, showing off its features like a real estate agent.

"I can't sit at the table!" Andrew announced at a volume more appropriate for a lecture hall. Then, even louder, he shouted, "I *can't* go outside!" The man emphasized that one negative word in both comments with bitterness and disgust. Lastly, with a pained grimace, he added, "I can't even use the goddamned bathroom on my own!"

He grew eerily calm then, and with the back-to-back comparison of everything else he just shouted, his next words were more profound at a whisper. "I can't feel my legs from my hips down to my toes."

A swell of emotion hit when his words registered. Shocked didn't really cover it. I felt guilty for rambling about eating damn sandwiches when the whole time he was waiting to tell me this startling fact.

Why had he waited this long to tell me?

"Wha-Wha— What do the doctors say?" I finally spluttered while choking on the pain I felt for him. The pain I saw on his crumpled face as he admitted those things.

"What do you think they say?" He scoffed bitterly, and I

reared back. I knew he was upset, and of course it all made so much more sense now, but I didn't deserve to be his whipping post.

So, in hopes of bringing the tension around us down to a manageable level, I calmly said, "Listen, I'm not trying to upset you. I'm trying to understand what we're dealing with here. What kind of work we have ahead of us."

"What's this us?" he mocked, and I cocked my head to the side, trying to reconcile this one-hundred-eighty-degree change from the loving man who had greeted me not ten minutes before. The man who couldn't get enough of me and the smell he missed so much. But that ugly tone he just took with me really pissed me off.

"Do you think I'd walk out that door because of what you just told me?" I asked angrily. "Firstly," I continued, not letting him actually answer the question. I strode back toward his bed with a good amount of hurt fueling my frustration. "I care about you. Do you not get that? That isn't turned on and off based on inconsequential details."

"Inconsequential?"

"Secondly," I listed, refusing to be deterred. "What kind of human would that make me? Do you think so little of me?"

That was the possibility that stung the most. How could he not know unequivocally that I would stick it out alongside him regardless of a challenge like this? Whether the paralysis was permanent or temporary, it didn't change the man I was falling for.

Though, if he didn't recalibrate the tone he was taking with me, I'd have to rethink my conviction.

Andrew sighed heavily and studied his folded hands resting in his lap. He went through a couple of cycles of deep breathing, and I could appreciate he was regrouping in what I prayed was an effort to not spew any more venom my way.

"I'm so sorry, baby," he finally whispered.

"Sorry? What was that?" I asked, hand propped on my hip with a lot of sass. I gave him a quick wink to let him know I was trying to lighten the air in here.

He couldn't contain the slow grin that spread across his sinful lips. Instantly my stomach clenched, remembering the talented mouth I was staring at.

"Who would've known you're such a ballbuster under all that fluff?"

This time, when I went back to his bed, I didn't stop until I was lying beside him. I needed his embrace as much if not more than he needed mine. I hated arguing. With anyone. But shouting at each other was so unproductive when the true emotion needing to be addressed was fear.

When I was settled in his arms, I laid my head on his chest and listened to his strong heartbeat. "Please, Andrew. Tell me what your doctors expect for your recovery, unless you absolutely don't want to talk about it. Then I will respect your wishes. But you have to know, you can't get rid of me with a few ill-mannered comments. I'm in it for the duration, man."

"Ill-mannered, huh? Don't tell my mother. She and Mara will gang up on me and torture me as punishment," he said and kissed the side of my head.

I looked up to find his lips with mine and pressed into him. We kissed slowly, passionately, for a few minutes until I finally pulled back and asked, "Who is Mara?"

Thinking it would be one of his mother's friends, since I knew he didn't have siblings, I was surprised to hear it was the physical therapist assigned to his case. A pang of jealousy shot through me, and I instantly shut that shit down.

In the past, I'd had an ugly jealousy streak based on my own insecurities. There was no room for those immature feelings or accusations in our relationship. I knew that would be another benefit of dating an older man. No game playing. Or at least no childish, destructive game playing. Now...if he wanted to play some *naughty* games, I'd be on board for that.

"What's this grin, Ms. Farsey? You look like you're up to something in here." He tapped my temple while we lay nose to nose.

"Oh, busted. I was thinking naughty, sexy thoughts. Just being close to you ignites my core. It's so amazing and unfamiliar. I think that makes these feelings even more exciting."

We spent the next hour in bed like that. Chaste kissing naturally led to desperate groping and making out. We giggled in between naughty promises and sincere declarations. By the time I was humping his leg with his enthusiastic encouragement, we were both panting like we'd run a marathon.

Without warning, the door to his room swung open, and I leaped off the bed like I'd been jolted with an electrical current.

"Smooth, darling," Andrew teased while I did a quick once-over to smooth down my dress.

"Oh, dear, I guess I should've knocked. My apologies," Mrs. Chaplin said and walked over to her son. "How are you feeling, dear? Besides the obvious?"

I was so thankful I was watching their exchange, because I saw the quick wink and mischievous grin she shot her son. I still felt like a teenager getting caught by my folks, although my dad would've dragged the boy out by the collar of his shirt and not sneaked an approving nod.

Guess that was the difference between forty-two and sixteen, though. Really, his mother should be the embarrassed one here for not knocking before entering her adult son's room. Good God, what if we'd been doing more than we were?

"Maye, dear!" she said when she finally faced me. "How are you? How's the arm?"

"Good, thank you. Just had a checkup this morning, and the doctor said it's healing nicely. Might be able to get this monstrous thing off in about a month. I might have to start hitting the gym with my twin and just work the other side. I think my shoulder is getting buff from lugging this thing around. I'm going to be completely lopsided by the time they saw it off."

Yep. I was rambling.

Regardless, the woman gave me a kind smile and turned her attention back to her son. "Has Mara been by yet? I wrote down some questions for her about home accommodations."

"Mom," Andrew said, and I didn't miss the hint of warning in his tone. He gave her an infinitesimal shake of his head, and the room fell awkwardly silent.

"I can go find a vending machine and get some drinks... For lunch," I stammered uncomfortably. Maybe he wanted to speak to her in private about that topic. I definitely felt like an interloper after the way he shut down her enthusiasm.

"No, don't leave," Andrew nearly barked.

With widened eyes, I looked at the man, wondering what the hell had come over him since his mom arrived.

"Sorry, baby," he said and forced his features to seem more relaxed. "That came out rougher than intended. Please don't go. Why don't we try to get some work done? If we can prove to Dean McCallister that we can work even while I'm stuck in here, maybe he won't put the kibosh on the internship program."

"Ohhhkaaay," I drew out cautiously. I wanted him to hear the trepidation in my response, because we were definitely going to be addressing these unnecessary mood shifts.

There was no way he'd get away with saying I misunderstood, or he was tired, or whatever bullshit reason he might try to use. I'd heard what I heard. And it happened twice already in the short time I was in his room.

Warning flares went off in the back of my mind. It wasn't fair to assume he would try to gaslight me when he hadn't pulled that abusive tactic with me once. That was Joel's bit, and Andrew didn't have to pay penance for that jackass's mistakes.

Nope. Not fair at all.

So while his mother set up camp in the corner of the room, I sat at the foot of Andrew's bed with my laptop perched on my legs. Together, we started creating a proposal for a grant offered by a national organization with very deep pockets. This was the one I had discovered the week we began. They were interested in giving money to groups or individuals doing research in psychological therapies for people with mental health diagnoses. The mission lined up perfectly with the new curriculum of the psychology department's graduate program. If we could secure a grant of that magnitude, the university's program could be expanded in so many ways.

After we ate the lunch I brought, Mara, the physical therapist, knocked softly before entering.

"How's my favorite professor today?" she asked with a lyrical voice you could listen to for hours.

"I'm amazing," Andrew said while giving me a wink.

"And this must be the lovely Maye who smells like

morning glories," she said and nudged him with her elbow.

Interesting. He'd only been at this facility a few days. How much one-on-one time did these two share?

"The one and only," he said with a warm smile. "But you need to stay quiet now before you give away all the things I let slip while you torture me every day."

"Oh now, wait a minute," I said playfully while clearing my things off his bed. I wasn't sure how much of their session was done there, and I didn't want to be in the way. "This sounds like information I should know."

Mara gestured as though she locked her lips closed tight and tossed the key over her shoulder. We all chuckled, and I put my computer in my bag. It was getting late, and from what both Andrew and his mom had told me, this girl would tire him out with her exercises.

"Darling," I said, and leaned down to kiss him. "I'm going to go. I know you'll be tired when the taskmaster here is done with you, and I'm really happy with what we accomplished today. I may work on the application more from home, if you're okay with that? You can always check everything before we submit."

"I'm sad to see you go, though. Will you come see me again soon?"

I tilted my head to one side and said, "You couldn't make me stay away. And now we have a goal other than getting you out of here."

We kissed briefly, and I stood up, but he grabbed my hand and tugged me back. Against my lips he said, "I wish you could stay. We have unfinished business, you know."

My grin couldn't be contained after we kissed one last time. "I'll see you tomorrow, okay? Maybe a little earlier if you're up for it. I won't have a doctor's appointment taking up most of my morning, so we can get even more accomplished."

"I can't wait to get out of this place. When I do, you're coming over and spending the night. Better yet, the weekend," he announced, as though we were the only two people in the room.

With a shy giggle, I darted my gaze to his mother to see if she was listening. If she was, she played it off like a pro and stayed busy with her sewing.

"Bye, Mrs. Chaplin. Maybe I'll see you tomorrow!"

"Oh, dear, are you leaving? Listen, let me walk out with you. I could use a stretch, and then Mara can really dig in here."

What was I going to say to her offer? I certainly didn't need an escort. It was broad daylight, and we were in a lovely area. By the size of the bag she slung over her shoulder, she looked like she was taking a month-long trek, not a stroll to the parking lot.

"Do you have the kitchen sink in there?"

She chuckled. "Big enough, right? I just like having options while sitting with him. I have my sewing, a few romance novels, a crossword puzzle book. You know, the essentials."

We chatted until we came to my car parked along the curb in front of the building. "Well, this is me," I announced and motioned to the sedan Shep and I shared.

"Please forgive me if I'm overstepping, dear," Mrs. Chaplin said while looking very serious.

"I'm sure you're fine. Please, speak your mind," I invited and immediately felt my nerves kick online. Was she about to tell me something he'd been holding back about his recovery? In those few seconds while the woman gathered her thoughts, I had at least twenty of my own and less than a third were positive.

"Thank you for spending time with my son. The difference in his mood today compared to every other day is hard to put into words. I know the two of you are a new thing, but I hope it sticks. You know?" She shifted the large bag from her shoulder to in front of her feet.

"I wouldn't be any place else. You're right. This is very new between us, well—as far as a romantic relationship. He probably told you I was a student of his this past semester." I smiled and marveled how life changed from day to day.

"Yes, and just so you know, that doesn't bother me. The age difference, I mean."

"Oh," I said, surprised she would so boldly mention that detail. "I— I'm glad." Not sure how else to respond to that, I waited for her to wrap up our little girl talk.

"You're a very mature young woman. He's lucky to have you. But that's what I really wanted to talk about, dear. I've seen the mood swings since the day I arrived and he regained consciousness."

"Has anyone addressed it? From what I know about his personality, he's not a volatile man. Granted, I don't know him all that well yet, but from what I do know..." I paused there, trying to label the behavior as gently and accurately as possible. "Well, it's concerning."

"His team of doctors said it's pretty normal when a patient has head trauma. From the injuries he has, they think the car hit him, and he then hit his head on the pavement when he went down. Most patients recover from it, but for some, it's something they have to learn to live with."

Feeling uncomfortable now with the amount we were discussing his condition and recovery, I wanted to change the subject. Or better yet, say goodbye and drive away, leaving the guilt and the elderly woman there on the spot.

"Are you okay?" she asked. Apparently I wasn't masking my discomfort quite as well as I'd thought.

Best to be honest...

"I feel uncomfortable talking about him out here"—I gestured to the building—"instead of in there. With him." Thinking of his outburst today when he finally told me that he couldn't feel his legs piled on the guilty feelings.

"Oh, I'm sorry, dear," Mrs. Chaplin said while clutching my forearm without the cast. "I didn't mean to make you uncomfortable."

"No, it's fine. It's just that today—well, no, since this happened—he hasn't been very open with me about what his prognosis is. Today was the first time I heard." I swallowed hard as tears filled my eyes. God, I couldn't even say it aloud.

"The paralysis?" she finished for me as I nodded and swiped the tears rolling down my cheeks freely now.

"I didn't know," I repeated for some reason.

"They really believe it's temporary. When the swelling goes down around the spinal cord, they suspect he will regain use of his lower half. But trying to keep my son optimistic will be the real challenge." She still managed a warm smile for me after saying all that, and I tried to return the expression but came up short.

She pulled me into a fierce hug, and I awkwardly returned her effort. Damn cast was a real hindrance. "Sorry," I muttered into her shoulder when I clunked her hip with the thing.

We straightened then, and she held me by the shoulders. "This is what I really wanted to talk to you about when I walked out here with you."

I tilted my head a bit. "What is?"

"Can I count on you to help keep his spirits up? He needs all the positivity he can get right now, and I know you're the brightest spot in his world. Will you please help me ensure he recovers from this and doesn't spiral into a pit of depression and anger?"

"Yes, yes, of course. I'll do whatever I can do. I care for him deeply. It's all happening so fast, but he's such an incredible man, you know? Such a perfect match for me in every way possible." I was gushing about my feelings for her son and needed to shut my damn mouth or I'd come off as an infatuated girl.

"Good. It's settled, then. We're all team Andrew. And believe me, there may be days he doesn't like it, but together, we can get him back on his feet. Literally." She beamed while summarizing our plan, and I had to giggle at her enthusiasm. The love this woman had for her son was so touching, I started to get choked up all over again.

"I better get back in there. I really did want to speak to Mara about some accommodations that need to be made in his house so we can get him out of here. The sooner the better for all of us."

"Thank you, Mrs. Chaplin," I said and gave her another hug.

"No, thank you. And please, call me Millie."

"All right. See you tomorrow, Millie."

CHAPTER FIFTEEN

ANDREW

Two weeks later, I signed my discharge papers releasing me from the orthopedic rehabilitation facility that I called home for nearly a month. In total, I lost thirty-eight days of my life recovering from some asshole's twisted version of revenge. Yet here I was, still desperately trying to focus on the positive.

My mother and Maye were driving me crazy with their constant upbeat rah-rah attitudes, but I knew they meant well. I would always cherish the hours the beautiful, intelligent, witty, and ambitious young woman devoted to not only my recovery and mental health stability but also my general well-being. If I added up all the time she'd spent lying with me, talking with me, and just being silly so I wouldn't spend too much time in my own head, we compacted a six-month period of regular dating into the past few weeks.

I'd regained some feeling in my legs, and the doctors still believed I'd make a full recovery. Now that I was headed home, Mara sent me off with a program of exercises to do daily. She was wise enough to issue her demands right in front of Maye and Mom, so there would be no skipping workouts once I got home.

Home.

One word never had more appeal. Well, maybe one. *Maye.*

All I had to do was say her name or hear it spoken by another, and happiness enveloped me. There hadn't been another time in my life when I was so at peace. It seemed like a strange takeaway after being run down by a vehicle, but life worked in funny ways.

There was a warrant issued for Joel Higgins. Footage from three different security cameras in that parking lot was used to place his car at the scene the night I was hit and identified him as the driver.

Now, because of his uncontrolled jealousy, the guy was facing attempted voluntary manslaughter charges.

The only problem was the kid took off from the scene of the accident, and the authorities still hadn't located him. With Baja being so close, there was suspicion that he had crossed the border within a week of the incident. The police were still trying to obtain security camera footage from the border checkpoints to see if they could track him into Mexico.

He would get what was coming to him one day. One way or another, he'd pay for what he did. Best of all, I still had the girl. And I had no intention of letting her go. Because I'd been confined to a bed for the past month, we'd spent so much time just talking. I felt like I knew her on a deeper level than I'd ever known any other woman I'd dated.

She was so genuine and honest, and when I asked her questions, she always gave it to me straight. I loved that about her. Honestly, there were so many things I loved about her, I couldn't imagine a day going by without her in it. Several times I was tempted to invite her to move into my home when I was discharged, but I feared I'd spook her by rushing things.

Two weeks ago, I convinced her to start using my car as her own. It was ridiculous that she had to bargain for the use of the vehicle she shared with her twin. Plus, my car was just sitting in my driveway collecting dust and leaves. There were selfish reasons for my generosity too. With transportation at her disposal, she could spend every day at the hospital with me.

"I'm going to miss it here," she said the morning of my discharge as we looked around the room for the last time.

I tipped my head to the side in a *be serious* kind of way, and she immediately defended her comment.

"I'm serious. We've been in our own little cocoon here, and I've loved spending so much time together. Plus, the staff," she added with affection. "I'm going to miss seeing all of them, too."

Her heart was so big and so generous, it made me care for her that much more. Her eyes were filled with unshed tears as she said goodbye to all the regulars who had helped on my road to recovery.

"Don't be sad now," my attending physician told her. "Andrew will have plenty of follow-up appointments in the next few months. You'll still see us. Just because he's going home doesn't mean his recovery is over."

Yeah, thanks for that reminder, Doc.

"Positive. I'm staying positive," I reminded myself.

Maye squeezed my hand and looked down to where I sat in the facility's wheelchair. "What did you say?"

My mother pushed me toward the exit while Maye walked alongside, gripping my hand possessively. On the opposite shoulder, she carried a large duffel with the belongings I'd accumulated over the duration of my stay.

Her cast was fully decorated now. People signed it and drew random pictures on the blue fiberglass, and tomorrow she had an appointment to finally have the thing removed.

Once I was settled in the passenger seat of the car, Mom in the back and Maye behind the wheel, I asked her about the appointment.

"Are you excited about tomorrow? Getting the cast off?" I added when she looked at me with confusion.

Her shoulders dropped low after she put the car in drive. "No. They moved the appointment to Friday, so now I have to wait a few more days."

"That sucks. Why did they reschedule?" I asked, just making small talk as we made our way home.

She shrugged. "Not sure why. I didn't ask, and they didn't say. I've had it on for this long. A few more days will be fine."

I stared at her with longing while she drove. She knew I was looking at her, though, because she sneaked glances my way when traffic permitted. Each time she'd smile a little wider until finally she reached over and gave my knee a squeeze.

"What are you looking at, Professor?" she asked in that throaty, sultry tone her voice took on when aroused.

"The most beautiful woman I've ever seen," I said and brought our joined hands to my lips and softly kissed her knuckles.

She tilted her head and grinned as though I were making a joke. "Oh, you're so full of charm, aren't you?"

Leaning all the way across the armrest that separated our seats, I spoke right beside her ear so my mother wasn't part of the exchange. "I'm definitely full of something, and I can't wait to show you what."

The flush that spread across her chest and up her neck to her cheeks was intoxicating. I wanted to cause that same reaction over and over again. Preferably while inside her, because I was positive I'd never get tired of seeing the way she physically responded to me.

I slid back to my own seat and discreetly adjusted the erection pushing on my slacks. My legs weren't back to full capacity, but my cock sure as hell was, and I could not wait to get Maye alone.

We'd talked about our fantasies, and our general likes and dislikes in the bedroom. We'd covered so many topics by that point, I knew our first time would be incredible. I'd never been forced to have such detailed conversations about sex with a woman before bedding her. The anticipation had reached a crescendo for us both, and we couldn't wait for my mom to go to bed that evening.

Maye already planned on spending the night, and we talked about it casually around my mom so she wouldn't make a scene when the time came. At my age, and in my own home, I didn't need her permission to have overnight guests. I just didn't want her voicing her opinion if she disagreed and made my baby uncomfortable or dampened the magical night we had planned.

Two nights ago, while Maye lay in my arms in my twin-sized hospital bed, I spoke low in her ear and described what I had planned for her. For her body. After about ten minutes of that particular bedtime story, I slid my hand into her panties and found the wettest pussy I'd ever felt. I got her off with my fingers and dirty talk, and the memory had been taunting me ever since.

Currently I was using a walker to get around. The damn thing was bulky and cumbersome, but until I built up stamina and fully regained my balance, it was a necessary evil.

Walking through my front door was more emotional than I expected. Maye and my mom had worked in shifts to keep the place clean and ready for my return, and I was overwhelmed with gratitude and appreciation for them and life in general. It would be dramatic to say I had a brush with death or worried that I'd never see the place again, but something about the experience gave me a fresh outlook on being alive.

A big part of my brighter attitude was the amazing woman at my side. There was so much to look forward to in a future that included her. When I didn't respond to her welcome-home wishes, she stopped right in front of me and waited for me to meet her stare. My mother shuffled past us and continued down the hall to the guest room.

Tears pooled in my eyes and tied my words into knots. Maye scooped my hands into hers and waited for me to speak. A tear spilled over and streaked down my cheek, and she tenderly swiped it away.

"Oh, honey. What's all this?" she asked gently.

Finally able to speak, I told her the words that had been repeating on a loop in my mind for the past week. "I love you so much."

She stepped into my arms, and I buried my face in her thick hair. Again, I said, "I fucking love you, Maye."

"I love you too. I haven't seen you this emotional, even after everything you've been through. What brought this on? Not that there's anything wrong with crying. Hell, I do it at least once a week, myself." She sneaked me a quick wink, and I chuckled and pulled her against me again.

"I'm not really sure. Walking through my front door, it was so overwhelming. I feel so much gratitude for being alive. For being healthy enough to recover from something like what just happened. But most of all, for having someone as incredible as you to share every day with. Yeah, it's all just overwhelming."

Maye tugged me toward the kitchen so I could rest on one of the stools at the island. Quietly, she said, "That was all very beautifully said. Thank you for sharing with me. You know, it would probably sound weird to other people, but I've enjoyed this past month."

I nodded in agreement—or understanding, rather—of the sentiment she expressed.

"Getting to know you, spending so much quiet time together," she continued while looking down and shuffling her feet. "I think I knew I was in love with you that very first day I lay in your bed with you. It's been hard not blurting it out because I didn't want you to think I was just a silly girl." She rolled her eyes and looked every bit her tender age. "Getting lost in my feelings. I didn't want to scare you off. I'm so thankful you were honest about how you were feeling."

With my arms extended, I invited her to stand between my knees, and we held each other that way for long moments.

"You smell so good," I muttered with my head resting on her chest. I looked up to find her attentive blue eyes watching me. Boldly, I told her, "I can't wait to peel this pretty dress off you, baby." Then, I let out a tortured groan because just the mere mention of seeing her naked made my cock swell.

"Do you think your mom is in for the night?" she asked.

Could I dare dream that she was as anxious to be alone as I was?

"Probably. I mean, we didn't hide the fact that we had some celebrating planned tonight."

"Do you want something to eat before we head?" She motioned with her chin down the hallway.

If she were too shy, I'd be happy to fill in the words. "To our bed?"

Her grin doubled in size, and she nodded. My words must have taken a second to register though because she tilted her head to the side and asked, "Our?"

"Damn straight, that's what I said. I want you to make yourself at home here. Hell, if I had my way, we'd be planning the move from your parents' house to here."

"Oh, Andrew," she said, and I couldn't really read the tone. It sounded like a protest. Maybe a warning? "You want me to move in here with you?"

"I would love that. When you're ready, of course. In the meantime, please make yourself at home. You can leave some things here so you don't have to worry about packing a bag every night."

She was quiet then, and I worried I pushed for too much too soon. I could feel her nervous energy sparking all around her body as she fussed with the tie at her hip that held her dress closed.

I captured her busy hands in mine and waited for her to look at me. "I'm sorry if I'm pushing you. I won't mention it again until you bring it up. But know that is what I want, and it is a standing offer." The air was heavy between us now, and I was kicking myself for potentially ruining the mood. "Babe..." I began to say just as she spoke at the exact same time.

"I want that too."

We both laughed. Then again, at the same time, both said, "You go."

"Ladies first. I insist." I swept my hand out in front of us as if clearing a path for her.

"I'd like to introduce you to my parents. Would you be okay with that? They're not old-fashioned, necessarily. I mean, you've met my mom, but my father is very protective of his daughters." Her smile warmed even more as she spoke about the man who raised her.

"I think he has always had certain expectations about how we should be respectful in his home with regard to our dating practices." Maye chuckled and added, "Although, with my two older sisters, a lot of those expectations were completely trampled on."

"I would love to meet them. You've talked so reverently about them. I'm sure they're lovely people."

Surely Maye had explained to them how we'd met, so they shouldn't be caught off guard by our stark age gap.

"Why don't we have them over for dinner?" I offered. "We can cook together."

"You would do that?"

"Oh, baby, I would do anything for you."

CHAPTER SIXTEEN

ANDREW

Both showered, teeth brushed and ready for bed, we worked together to pull the heavy quilt down to the footboard. Technically, summer was coming to an end, but the warm weather usually lasted well into October in Southern California.

Maye was quiet as we got into bed. The queen-size mattress seemed enormous after spending so many hours together in my hospital bed.

"Come closer, baby. You're much too far away for my plans." Even I could hear the low register my voice dipped into the minute we dimmed the lights. My dick was already at full attention knowing the pleasure about to unfold.

"The bed seems so big now, doesn't it?" she marveled, and I smiled, having just had the same thought.

"We could sleep on the couch?" I offered in a serious tone.

She shot her wide, navy eyes my way, and I couldn't hold the ruse.

"Joking. I'm joking, baby. But I was just thinking the same thing about what we're used to sharing."

I'd already had enough small talk. If I didn't get my fingers on her flesh, I'd lose my mind. "Lay here. Let me look at you first."

She shimmied into place on her back and stared up at me with darting eyes.

"Don't be nervous, okay? If you ever want me to stop, just tell me, okay? But that's the only way I'll know you don't like something. You have to tell me."

"What are you planning on doing that you're saying that?" She gulped. My attempt to ease her nerves seemed to ramp them up instead.

"So many things. I'm just deciding where to start," I warned with a devilish grin, and she sucked in a breath. I moved to hover over her, my arm and shoulder muscles stronger than ever. I was having to overcompensate for the weakness in my legs with upper body strength, so the past month of Mara's vicious regimen had me very toned.

"But first, these are definitely in the way," I said and flipped up the bottom hem of her pajama top. After her shower, she dressed in a silky menswear-style pajama set. The palest shade of lavender against her long blond hair reminded me of fairy tales.

I straddled her waist and sat back on my heels so I could slowly unbutton her top. Button by button, I slowly exposed more of her delicate skin. Holding her stare while I spread the two halves wide, I saw her trepidation.

"I'm not going to hurt you," I whispered.

"I know. I don't know why I'm so nervous." She smiled awkwardly. "I think I'm afraid of disappointing you. You have a lot more experience here than I do."

"But you already know what an amazing teacher I am," I said with a wink. "I won't mind mentoring you."

Unexpectedly, she burst out laughing.

I tried my best stern expression, but she just giggled more.

"Ms. Farsey," I warned, but I caught her silliness and ended up chuckling too.

"That was so cheesy, dude," she said and pushed my chest.

Quickly I snatched her by the wrist and widened my eyes. All laughing stopped as I leaned in closer to her sweet lips.

"Cheesy?" I said right before crashing my mouth into hers.

Maye moaned beneath me, and that one sexy sound evaporated all playfulness and all the previous tension from the air. Now, lust and need enveloped us as our kissing grew feverish.

"Andrew," she moaned again, and this time way louder than before.

I put a small amount of space between our mouths, and she tried chasing me for more. With one stern look, she collapsed flat to the mattress and sucked in a ragged breath.

"Easy, baby. No more noise at that volume, or my mother will be knocking on that door." I thumbed over my shoulder.

Adorably, she leaned past my body to get a visual on the door. That move made me chuckle, and she furrowed her brows.

"I'd be mortified," she whispered, and I agreed with a quick dip of my chin.

"Let's not test the experience. Do you need me to gag you for good measure?" I cocked my brow, and my cock jumped at the same time. Apparently, every part of my anatomy liked that image.

"No, I'll be good. Don't stop," she whispered and clutched my braced forearms. "Please, don't stop."

"No." I shook my head slowly, left to right. Left to right again. "We're just getting started." I backed down her legs and hooked my fingers into the waistband of her pj's and tugged. "What the—" I cut my profanity off when I realized there was a drawstring standing between me and what I wanted. *Needed.*

"Untie these fucking things," I growled and waited for Maye's brain to catch up to what was going on.

Her feminine fingers fumbled with the drawstring until her pants finally gave way when I tugged. With an aggressive *swoosh*, the pants joined her top on the floor. Maye propped herself up on bent forearms and gave me a hungry look.

"What about you?" she whispered.

"We'll get there. Promise. But right now, I don't trust myself not to sink right into you if I take my dick out." I pushed her by the shoulders, and she fell flat to the mattress with a yip.

"Quiet now," I reminded her and positioned my body between her thighs. "Lie back and feel me love this incredible pussy." I ran a firm stroke up the entire length of her leg just to the juncture of her thighs. I repeated the motion over and over, always nearing her pussy but shying away at the last moment.

Maye held her breath every time I got close to touching the place we both wanted, then exhaled in frustration when I didn't give her what she wanted. I planned to keep up the torture until she begged me.

Thankfully, I didn't have to wait very long. After about three more passes up her shapely calves and thighs, she cried out my name laced with need.

"Andreeewwww," she moaned, and I knew she was right where I wanted her. Hot, vulnerable, and desperate. "Please."

"Please what, baby?"

"Touch me. No more teasing. I'm going crazy here."

"Does it ache?" I taunted. "Do you want my touch so bad it hurts?"

"Yes. Yes, God, please." She arched her back, and her hair tumbled in waves onto the pillow like a golden waterfall. "Please, I need you."

"I need you too, baby." I kissed the inside of one knee. "Let your knees fall open wide."

Well, that made her sit up like her dad just busted in through the door.

"Andrew," she breathed, looking at me with the most unsure expression.

"What is it, baby?" I purred and ran my hand up her leg.

"Why— What— What are you going to do?" she stammered.

Every part of me wanted to chuckle at her reaction. But I knew she was feeling self-conscious about what I asked her to do, so now would not be a good time to laugh.

"I want to look at you. Memorize the way you look before I memorize the way you taste. It's just us here. By the end of the night, my hands, lips, and tongue are going to explore every inch of your spectacular body. There's no reason to feel self-conscious."

Her blank stare just egged me on more.

"Lie back and show me your pussy, Maye." Now my voice took the *don't fuck with me* tone I used in the classroom.

Her eyes widened comically before she collapsed back to the mattress. I could hear her muttering while she lay there but couldn't quite make out what she was saying.

I let it slide—this time. I was too ramped up to wait a second longer.

When I spread her pussy open, she jolted at the contact.

"Ssshhh," I admonished. "I'm going to make it so good, baby. Relax and feel me."

After that last instruction, I went to town. I ate her pussy as if I couldn't get enough. Every swipe of my tongue took her higher and higher. She had both hands gripped in my hair, and it definitely felt more like keeping me in place than pushing me away. When I slid a finger into her opening, she keened so loudly that I shot my eyes across the length of her body to hers in warning, and she slapped her palm across her mouth.

She was so damn tight and wet. I was in danger of coming right along with her.

"Give it to me, girl," I panted and picked up the pace of the invasion. "Come, baby."

Her undulating hips stilled, and she burst with a low moan that quietly escaped from behind her hand. I continued lapping at her folds until she pushed my face away from her sensitive flesh.

"Oh, shit, shit, Andrew. Too much. Too sensitive," she said between pants.

"Can you go again?" I encouraged—or maybe hoped.

Maye shook her head and invited me with open arms. "Come to me. I want to feel all of you."

I rolled off to her side to get a condom on. I hated the fucking things and hated the thought of anything between us while we made love even more. I wanted to feel her heat, her wetness, her fluttering walls in truth. I appeased myself with the thought that one day it would be that way. I planned on keeping this girl by my side, in my bed, in my life, for as long as she'd have me.

After suiting up, I lay on the bed beside my beautiful queen. I took her hand and encouraged her to climb on top. "Ride me, baby. It'll be easier on my legs with you on top."

She worried her bottom lip between her teeth and

admitted, "Oh, I don't know, Andrew. I've... I've never done it that way."

"We'll go slow. You sink down on me, and we'll find a pace that we can both deal with, okay?" I explained and prayed she'd go along with it. "Rub on me first, get me wet with that dripping pussy."

"Jesus..." she muttered.

I chuckled. "What?"

"The things you say. I'm just not used to it. I've only been with two other guys, and honestly, they were bumbling idiots compared to you," she said nervously while mounting me. I knew the chatter was her way of dealing with her nerves, so I just went with it.

"Stick with me, baby. I'll show you a whole new world," I promised. And yes, there was some smugness involved, but how could it be helped after the confession she'd just made?

I positioned my cock for her to slide down on, and we both moaned in unison when she took my full length.

"Oh my God. Feels so good."

"Lie down on me, baby. We'll just move here for a little bit."

She followed my guidance, and together, we rocked our bodies until we found a perfect rhythm.

"It feels so good," she breathed with eyes wide with wonder. "I had no idea."

"Yeah, it does. You're so full. So tight around me," I groaned, trying to hold on to my orgasm that was battering my balls for release. "Not going to last, though. It's so fucking warm inside your little body."

My own dirty talk was making it harder to hang on. Maye grew brave and sat up tall, still speared on my cock. She raised up just a few inches and slid back down, and I knew it was over. One more time with the same motion, and that's all it took. That little bit of friction sent my body over the edge. I felt the orgasm from my toes to the top of my head as I gripped her hips and thrust up into her, milking out every last drop into the condom.

"Wow, that was so hot," she said, looking down at me with a sexy smile. "Watching you fall apart like that. That could become addicting."

When I could speak again, I replied, "Anytime you want. Anytime at all."

We fell asleep in each other's arms. It had been a long day, and finally making love to the amazing woman beside me was the perfect ending.

CHAPTER SEVENTEEN

MAYE

The rich, dark, delicious scent of coffee woke me the next morning. I stretched beneath the covers and felt how delightfully sore my body was. Everywhere. The smile that spread across my lips couldn't be helped. Heck, I didn't even want to hide it. It had been so long since I felt this truly happy, I wanted to run around the block a few times shouting about it.

Life was complicated. It always was. You wouldn't think at my age I'd already feel so burdened, but it had more to do with my personality than anything. I've always liked things in measured, controlled portions. So when things became chaotic, as they often did by means I couldn't control, I was left to scramble and regroup.

Andrew was so much better at pivoting than I was. Granted, he usually did so with a scowl and some grumbling, but he wasn't left restless for days like I was when things didn't go according to plan.

Take the accident, for example. While he was angry and swore justice would be served, after a few days of adjusting, he set a new plan in place. He had spoken to the dean about the internship and scholarship program and assured the man we could continue our work even though he was laid up.

In the end, we were able to submit two grant proposals,

even after the timeline setback we suffered in those first days after he was hit. Now came the hard part—the waiting. It would take months for the grant applications to be reviewed and processed, but I was hopeful we'd have a decision before I was due to start the first semester of grad school.

Everything hinged on our grants being awarded. If we secured the money we applied for, my grad school tuition would be paid for. If we didn't, I'd have to scramble for financial aid. No matter what, I decided I wouldn't put further financial burden on my parents. I could apply for student loans and get a job to make the payments without involving them.

Working with Andrew had solidified my decision to follow this career path. The process was so rewarding in itself, and if the grants were awarded to the university, I'd feel even more satisfied.

Satisfied.

Now there was a word I really appreciated this morning too. Making love to Andrew last night was better than I could have dreamed. My past experiences didn't just pale in comparison—they were completely erased. No wonder Shepperd always extolled the values of an older man.

Jesus, the difference was night and day. Now that I had a taste of being intimate, though, I wanted to do it again. And again.

Where was that man of mine?

I quickly dressed and followed my nose to the source of that enticing coffee aroma. I had bite marks all over my body, so before going out to the kitchen and possibly running into Millie, I made sure I was appropriately covered.

And there he was, leaning against the counter, shirtless and glorious. His upper body was perfectly sculpted from all the exercises Mara had him doing. Fortunately, he was alone, so I nuzzled into his bare skin while circling my arms around his waist.

"Good morning, baby. How did you sleep?" he asked and kissed the top of my head.

"Better than I have in a long time. Do I smell coffee?" I asked while not wanting to let go of the embrace.

"Sit. I'll get you a cup," he offered, and I let him move about the kitchen at his own pace. He was really getting around better than I expected, even if he had to use the countertops for balance every now and then.

He slid a cup of coffee toward me and went back to the pot to refill his own. When he came back to stand near me, he said, "I could really get used to this. Seeing you well fucked and rested every morning."

I felt the flush of embarrassment warm my cheeks but thought I'd be bold with my reply. "I wouldn't mind doing that again. And again."

"Greedy girl," he teased with a wink. "However, I'd be more than happy to accommodate you, Ms. Farsey."

We stared at each other over our mugs for a long beat, heat and desire building just through our stares.

Finally, I cleared my throat. "So what do you have planned for the day? It feels weird having free time now that the grants have been submitted."

"That's what I was daydreaming about when you first walked in. All the things I want to do with you. Places I want to take you to, things I want to show you. I love this city for the many things right at our fingertips."

"I'm at your disposal, Dr. Chaplin. We just have to make sure you don't overdo it. We don't want to backslide. You know, there are things I've been wanting to say to you, things I've been giving a lot of thought to."

His face fell to a worried scowl. "I'm not sure I like the sound of that. Are you about to crush me here?"

"No, my God, no," I assured with a hand on his. "It's all good stuff, I promise. I'm so proud of you. Of how seriously you've taken your recovery and of how hard you're working to get back to pre-accident you. I know it hasn't been easy, and I know there have been times you've wanted to give up. I just think you're amazing, and I wanted to tell you that."

I heaved out a lungful of air and inwardly felt pretty proud of myself for getting all that out. I wasn't always comfortable expressing my feelings to other people. But Andrew mattered. This thing we were building mattered.

He pushed his way between my spread legs and bent lower so we were nose to nose. "Thank you, baby. For saying those things and being so incredibly supportive and patient with me. I've only been able to do the things you mentioned because I've had you in my corner. Even if you are a pushy nuisance at times." Again, he gave me one of those sexy winks he had perfected, and a rush of arousal shot through my whole body.

Nostrils flared, eyes wide, a little breathless. I could just imagine what he saw while watching my reaction to him. To his nearness. To his allure.

"Let's go back to bed for a while. It's the weekend. It's early still. And I want to get you naked again more than anything."

I stood when he backed up and took his outstretched hand. We both grabbed our coffee mugs and headed back down the hall to the master bedroom. Excitement spiked my pulse just remembering what last night was like and knowing it was all about to happen again.

"Maybe I should get a shower first. I mean, since we did all that last night..." I wasn't sure what else to say.

"No way. I want to smell your skin with me all over it," he growled low in my ear. "Your cunt from the last time I marked you."

It was the filthiest thing anyone had ever said to me, and I actually choked on my own response.

"Oh... Okay. Jesus, Andrew. You're a dirty old man. I had no idea."

"You haven't seen anything yet, baby." He waggled his brows and grinned. "Just wait. Arms up," he instructed, and I complied without giving a thought. He pulled my shirt over my head and tossed it to the floor behind him.

He sat on the edge of the bed and tugged me to stand between his legs, putting his face directly level with my breasts.

"Christ, these tits. So perfect," he muttered against my skin while planting tender kisses over my bra. His warm breath through the lace felt so good, I moaned when he sank his teeth into a pebbled nipple, and he shot me a warning glare.

"Quiet, lady. Or I'll have to stop," he threatened, but at the same time, he reached around my back and released my bra with one hand. He dragged the straps down my arms and let that fall to the floor too.

"My God, look at you. So perfect, so soft and smooth. This young body drives me wild, Maye. Your skin—fuck, your skin. I can't get enough of it."

While his praise was dirty in context, it filled me with such desire and confidence. Once again, I marveled at the difference between intimacy with him and the other awkward, bumbling experiences I'd had before.

How did I get this lucky? I wasn't sure what it was about

me that enthralled him so. I mean, I knew what he'd said. His compliments definitely weren't falling on deaf ears. But whatever drew him to me in the first place was a mystery. I decided to revel in the experience instead of doing my usual overanalyzation and self-sabotage.

A sharp nip to the underside of my breast brought my attention back to what he was doing. I gasped from the jolt of pain and then quietly moaned from the pleasure as his warm tongue soothed the bruise.

"Stay with me," he whispered between my breasts. "Right here with me."

I threaded my fingers through his messy bed hair and watched him make his way around my breasts with kisses and light bites. When he sucked a pert nipple deep into his mouth, I gripped his hair harder, causing him to moan too.

"Fuck, that feels so good," I whispered and dropped my head back. With that access to my throat, he slowly rose, kissing a trail of wet pleasure all the way up to my ear.

"Lie down, baby. I need to see all of you."

I followed his instructions and scurried onto the bed. He wasted no time tugging the loose joggers I wore down over my hips and ass and then tossed them to the pile of other discarded apparel.

"Excuse me, young lady." He smirked. "No panties? Is this a normal thing?"

"No." I grinned shyly. "I just threw on the pants this morning because you enticed me with coffee."

"This pussy is just for me now. Do you understand that? No one else sees it or touches it but me now."

I nodded eagerly, getting more and more aroused by his bossy demeanor.

"Tell me, baby," Andrew encouraged while lightly stroking the length of my leg and expertly avoiding the spot he was claiming.

"It's yours. Just yours." I gulped. It was becoming clear there would be no room for shyness with this man. He was confident with his skill and desire and wanted me to be in the same place.

"Spread your legs. Let me see all of you."

I hesitated then. The room was bright with the morning sun, and my nerves kicked in. I opened my legs a fraction, and he growled. I couldn't tell if that was a good sound or not, so I slid them apart a few more inches.

"Good girl. My God, you're so sexy. So beautiful," he praised while continuing the teasing strokes.

When his hand neared the juncture of my thighs, my pelvis rose off the bed involuntarily, as if chasing his touch. Begging for it.

"Are you wet?" he asked in a voice so low and rough, I shot him a look to ensure it was still the same man.

"I-I think so," I stuttered.

"Touch your cunt and find out," he said while his eyes held mine captive. "Do it, baby. Show me what I do to you."

Without grace, I dived my hand down between my thighs. Using just my index finger, I swiped through my folds that were indeed soaked, and I held the evidence out for him to inspect. I had no idea what had gotten into him this morning, but the whole scene was so freaking hot, I was ready to scream if I didn't get some relief.

He grabbed my wrist and brought my finger to his mouth and sucked my arousal from my skin. For a few minutes, he sucked and nibbled my finger, never breaking our gaze.

I finally cracked. "Andrew. Please," I asked with a few slow blinks of my lashes.

"That's so pretty, baby. The begging and those big baby-doll eyes. You're so fucking delicious. But I need to fuck you. Right now. Up on your hands and knees," he ordered.

I felt so self-conscious getting into that position. Whatever detail of my sex he hadn't seen before, he definitely could then. I bent my head low between my stiff arms, let my eyes drift closed, and waited. I felt him position himself at my entrance, and without any warning or instruction, he filled me to the hilt. His hips bumped my ass, he was so deep inside me.

I gasped so hard on the first thrust that I sputtered and coughed.

"Fuck, baby, you feel so good. How the hell is this pussy so tight and warm? My God, woman," he grunted in short staccato from behind me.

"Yes!" I called louder than intended as he pinched the flesh of my ass cheek. Though it was probably meant to quiet me, the arousing pain from the pinch made me yelp louder.

"Andrew," I chastised through gritted teeth. "I'm so close. Please," I babbled. No idea what I was begging him for, but I'd gladly put my pleasure in his hands if this was the result. Over and over, I'd give him what he wanted, because pleasing me seemed to be his number one desire.

He picked up the pace a bit and sank his fingers into the flesh of my hips to hold me in place for his thrusts.

After a minute of him bottoming out on every stroke, he growled, "I'm going to come, baby. Come with me. Right now, Maye, come with me."

After being so compliant to his demands, my body automatically heeded this request too. My orgasm washed through my entire body and gathered right where he stilled inside my channel. I burst with a loud moan. He groaned as my inner walls spasmed around his cock.

"Fuck, feels so good while I'm coming," he panted through his release. "Squeeze me, baby, take it all."

Jesus...the man was a beast this morning, and I loved every second of it. Plain and simple, I loved him.

We fell to the mattress and regulated our breathing while holding each other in an intimate embrace.

"You are a maniac, man. I'm not sure I can walk right now," I said and tapped the tip of his nose with my index finger.

"You're not actually complaining though, are you?" he began with a smug tone and ended the comment looking unsure of himself. Interesting how no matter how old the man, their egos could be just as fragile.

I planted a soft, lingering kiss to his scruffy jaw and vowed, "Absolutely not."

"Did I hurt you? You drive me crazy when I'm inside you. I don't know what came over me," he said with a hint of wonder.

I had to chuckle at the tone he used. "It was perfect. You're perfect."

We lay in bed for a while. Talking and kissing and just existing. It was one of the best days already, and it wasn't even ten a.m. I got lost in thought eventually, and Andrew studied me carefully. He finally cracked and asked if something was bothering me.

"No. Nothing at all."

"You got so quiet. You get this far-off look when you're really contemplative. I'm starting to recognize when you're deep in your head."

"How did this happen?" I asked in response.

"How'd what happen?"

"This. You and me. I feel like I'm going to wake up and find out it's all been a really long dream."

"No, baby, it's very real. As for how it happened? I'm not really sure of that myself. But here we are. I've never felt so connected to a woman before. Ever. There's something very special about you, Maye Louise. All I can do is hope you will let me continue to love you and honor you. From there, we'll have to see where things take us. You know?"

"I love you too. So much, Andrew. It scares me how fast these feelings came on. But, like you said, here we are."

"Let's do this," he offered, and I was his rapt audience. "We'll take it one day at a time. We don't have to rush things. And we'll promise to be honest with each other, communicate through the tough stuff, and you...never wear panties again."

"Oh my God." I batted at his shoulder. "I thought you were being serious."

"What?" he asked through his chuckle. "Totally serious. About all of it." He swept my hand into his and kissed my knuckles. "I don't want to go a day without you. How's that for serious?"

"I like that. Because I don't want to be without you either. The panties thing... We may have to negotiate that further."

"We'll see," he said, still with a mischievous grin.

And that's how our story started. We agreed to take it one day at a time and see where life would take us.

What more could a girl ask for?

ACKNOWLEDGMENTS

Thank you to the Waterhouse Press team, who has lent their time and individual talents to make my words shine. Special thanks to Scott Saunders, who sweats every detail and gives my words and ideas the polish they need. Shout out to the Waterhouse proofing, copyediting, and formatting teams. Thank you for your keen eye and attention to detail.

Thank you to the talented ladies on my personal team. Megan Ashley, Amy Bourne, and Faith Moreno—a million thank yous for the daily efforts you put forth to keep me on track. I couldn't do any of this without you.

As always, thank you, readers. Without you, stories would go untold. I appreciate each and every one of you.

ALSO BY VICTORIA BLUE

Shark's Edge Series *(with Angel Payne)*:
Shark's Edge
Shark's Pride
Shark's Rise
Grant's Heat
Grant's Flame
Grant's Blaze
*

Elijah's Whim
Elijah's Want
Elijah's Need
Jacob's Star
Jacob's Eclipse

Bombshells of Brentwood :
Accepting Agatha
Mentoring Maye
Saving Shepperd

Misadventures:
Misadventures with a Book Boyfriend
Misadventures at City Hall

Secrets of Stone Series *(with Angel Payne)*:
No Prince Charming
No More Masquerade
No Perfect Princess
No Magic Moment
No Lucky Number
No Simple Sacrifice
No Broken Bond
No White Knight
No Longer Lost

**For a full list of Victoria's other titles,
visit her at VictoriaBlue.com**

ABOUT VICTORIA BLUE

International bestselling author Victoria Blue lives in her own portion of the galaxy known as Southern California. There, she finds the love and life-sustaining power of one amazing sun, two unique and awe-inspiring planets, and four indifferent yet comforting moons. Life is fantastic and challenging and every day brings new adventures to be discovered. She looks forward to seeing what's next!

Visit her at VictoriaBlue.com